THE DRAGON

IN THE

LIGHTHOUSE

A DRAGON ROMANCE NOVEL BY

TIM BAIRD

ALSO AVAILABLE BY TIM BAIRD

Fantasy
The Dragon in the Whites
Washington's Dragon Hunter
Dragon Liberator
The Dragon in the Whites: Omnibus I

Science Fiction
Eggs in Two Baskets

Children's
Good Night Phobos, Good Night Deimos

Forthcoming Fantasy
The Dragon in the Whites: Omnibus II

This story is dedicated to anyone out there who enjoys a good romance story but regrets never finding one with dragonfire. This one is for you.

Foreword from the Author

Dragons of old have been called many things:

Tyrants
Killers
Stealers of gold
Kidnappers of princesses
Pillagers of castles

But can dragons love, and do they deserve it?

Read on to find out. Tim

CHAPTER I

Feeling the rough, well-worn grass of the field beneath her feet, Maggie billowed her wings out behind her to induce some drag. She began to slow, tilting herself further back to shift her body weight as she prepared to make contact. Cautiously probing the ground with her feet, she felt a ripping sensation in her heel as she brushed past a thorn bearing plant.

Cringing, she pushed aside the pain and mentally filed away a reminder to complain to the field manager about the thorns. Based on the pain in her right foot, she'd say an invasive population of barberry had crept into the runway, if her guess was correct.

Pushing down again, she allowed her heel claw to dig into the dirt and tear through the topsoil as she rapidly slowed to a halt. Bouncing from foot to foot, she dropped her tail to aid in the deceleration and flapped her wings several times in quick succession. Panting, she rushed to the side of the runway to catch her breath just in case another dragon was right behind her and looking to land.

It had been a long, boring flight from New York City to northern Vermont, but she had to come. At least according to her boss. That's literally all that he said. "You HAVE to go, Maggie! The client needs you! You're the dragonfire that keeps their money hot. Get on out there and make us proud!" She had protested that one of her

1

clutch was about to have her own eggs hatch and she wanted to be there in person to watch her grandchildren be born, but Argyle, her boss, would hear none of it.

From what she could tell, this whole meeting could have been handled through an email. They were always asking mundane questions about market growth and dividend reinvestments. Simple stuff that she could have easily explained over a ten-minute phone call or an email with some relevant documents and links to review. But who was she to argue? She was only the program manager overseeing the largest client at D-Trade with the longest tenure of any non-C-Level executive at the firm. She wasn't in the position to make these big decisions.

"Snap out of it, Maggie," she said to herself, shaking her wings behind her as she attempted to work the frozen kinks out of her limbs. She had flown at a higher elevation than normal to try to dodge some stagnant air and gain time in a strong current. While she had probably shaved off thirty minutes of flight time, she would end up needing twice that amount of time to warm up in her rental cave.

Shuffling over to the air traffic control perch off to the side, she mustered the strength to fly up the one-hundred feet to the platform where a pair of irritated-looking dragons sat glaring in her direction. Not sure what was wrong, she put on her best diffusive smile that she typically used when talking with clients who just watched their stock tank overnight. She knew an angry dragon when she saw one, but she wasn't sure why they were angry with her.

"Good evening, gentlemen," she started, injecting a cheerful tone into her voice, despite her exhaustion and desire to drift off to her lair for the night and fall asleep.

"Thanks for guiding me in. That double blast of fire really lit up the night and helped me to stay on course."

They both stared at her, clearly annoyed. The older of the two finally spoke up after an uncomfortable silence. "That wasn't a guidance blast, ma'am, that was a runway number indicator," he began. "As you'll know from the latest revision of the guidebook, Section III, Article II, Lines 1-26 clearly define that a dragon within one-thousand tail-lengths of the target airport will circle until they see a belch of fire indicative of their intended runway number."

"Guys, I'm sorry, I've been flying all night and I—" she tried to say.

"Excuse me, ma'am," he deadpanned. "Upon visual receipt of said fire belch, the incoming dragon is to then signal back with the same number of belches to indicate acknowledgement and ready all available crew to enable streamlined coordination with other incoming dragons and on-ground dragon personnel. It is all very simple. Do I make myself clear?"

Crossing her arms, the sound of the hardened scales rustling over each other as they rubbed in passing, she slowly scanned back and forth across the field. She purposely did it far more slowly than was necessary to help accent the dramatic effect of her annoyance. She was in full sarcasm mode now. And it usually ended up getting her in trouble.

"There are no other dragons coming in for a landing," she began. She looked down at the ground very slowly, panning side to side. "And you're the only jackasses here. So, who else was I trying to avoid and prepare for my obviously disastrous incoming?"

She leaned forward in the darkness to get a look at the

male dragon's name tag affixed to his chest. Not able to read it in the dark, despite her heightened visual acuity, she roared a small, yet still-pretty-hot gout of flame at his chest to illuminate the tag. "Huh, Dwight?"

An hour later, she hovered in the cool night air along the cliffside hotel reserved by her company prior to departure. It took her a while as her room was near the bottom where it was easier to reach by land creatures and therefore, cheaper. She had scanned the upper levels initially, but alas, she was given a bargain cave once again. They really knew how to stiff us on these trips to maximize profits, she thought to herself as she heaved the boulder back in place to close off the entrance.

Dropping her satchel to the stone floor, she reached inside for the watermelon she had stashed in there and made her way over to the pile of hay in the far end of the rocky enclosure. Spinning on one heel, she turned around and dropped into the soft, warm nest. The hotel was in a fairly crappy location, but the staff here did know how to make a pretty mean nest. If she woke up without getting any bug bites, she'd have to remember to tip them well.

Tossing the melon into the air, she flicked out her sharpest claw and quickly separated two thin slices of the watery delight and caught the remainder with her other hand. Popping the majority of the melon into her maw, she laid the two slices over her closed eyelids and hunkered in for the night.

CHAPTER II

"Good morning!" A distant voice called out beyond Maggie's dream.

Barely comprehending the presence of the rude entity intruding upon her slumber, she continued sleeping. Her snoring scantily missing a beat in its draconian drone.

"Good morning," the voice continued, this time emanating along with a sing-song tune. "Good morning! Doo doo doo. Bah bah bah bah, bah bah bah-bah! Good morning! Bah bah bah bah, bah bah bah-bah! It's a beautiful day!"

More awake now than she would have preferred to be at this point, Maggie rolled to her left and swung her massive, clawed palm blindly through the dim early morning air in the general direction from which she perceived the voice to be coming. Eyes still closed, she heard a cry for help as the wakeup call routine abruptly ended.

Cracking open one eyelid just enough to catch a glimpse of what had transpired, she gasped. Standing before her was a dazed human male buried to his knees in the dirt floor of the cavern.

"Oh dear!" she exclaimed to the semi-conscious human. I am so sorry!"

Swinging her legs out from under her curled self, she deftly moved from a sleeping position to one of kneeling as low as possible before the poor thing. She grabbed him around the waist with a single hand and gently plucked him from the fresh hole in the ground. Turning her head a little, she looked at the small being from several angles and noticed that his knees were abnormally bent and his head was slightly crooked to one side. Reaching back out, she gingerly gripped his feet and head with separate hands and slowly pulled him out straight. Hearing a tiny 'pop' as the wee creature's bones and ligaments snapped back into position, she smiled in earnest hope that it had worked. If the tiny being were to regain consciousness and look up at her, she wanted to convey a sense of comfort and ease.

The tiny thing finally opened its eyes and looked up into hers. And screamed. Dipping her head in dismay, she stood up and quickly got ready to leave. Gathering her paperwork for the day ahead while trying not to feel too badly about the blood-curdling emanations blasting from the tiny little human mouth, she scooped the creature up in one arm and flew down to the main office on the ground level. Walking through the entrance to the well-decorated cavern below, she gently placed a hand over the human's head to muffle the cries of pain.

"Good morning. How may I help you?" the clerk at the front desk inquired as Maggie approached, clearly trying hard not to look down at the mournful sounds coming out from under her hand.

"Hi there," Maggie began. "Sorry for the noise. I think that I broke your human," she whispered, leaning in closer to the other dragon in the hopes that some of the others mingling in the lobby for breakfast wouldn't overhear. She lifted her hand to see the trembling male laying in her palm, staring up at her in terror. He was about to scream again when she moved a hand in closer and rested a single claw on his lips, making a "shhh" sound.

"Oh my!" the clerk muttered. "How dreadful!" He reached out and picked up the tiny thing, gripping a leg between his thumb and forefinger claws.

"I know! I'm sorry," Maggie muttered. "What do I owe you?"

"For this?" the clerk questioned, motioning to the inverted creature. "Oh, nothing at all. These things happen." He flung the creature into a bin next to the desk. "We have plenty more out back."

"Oh, well, thank you, I really appreciate it. I hope that he is okay. I just couldn't fall asleep last night and was very restless even when I did. I was so tired when he started screeching and I didn't realize what I was doing."

"No worries at all, ma'am," the clerk said. "Will you be checking out this morning?"

"Yes."

"Name and room number?"

"It is Maggie, I mean, Magendron the Destroyer," she answered. "Sorry, I only use that stuffy old name for contracts and banking documents. And I was in Room 54."

"Very well," the clerk answered, going through the menus on his computer screen. Tapping a few more buttons, he finally said, "And you are all set. I've billed the remaining balance to your card on file. Our complimentary breakfast is available around the counter and is served until ten this morning. Enjoy and have a great day!"

Thanking the male and looking back over his shoulder toward the bin where the human had landed, Maggie made a quick pass through the dining cavern. She quickly scooped up a few snacks for the flight over to the client's office. While she had plenty of time for a larger sit-down breakfast, her stomach was in knots, and she couldn't fathom eating more than a few bland bites right now anyway. Tucking a smoked pig and a barrel of orange juice into her satchel, she exited the hotel and took to the sky. She would have preferred one of the live pigs, but she couldn't risk getting blood on her clean scales before meeting with the client. Her personal presentation was important, and she couldn't risk losing this account.

Soaring through the cool morning air, she reminded herself to enjoy the beauty of the moment and to take a deep breath from time to time. It wouldn't do to stress out on the little things in life if it meant missing out on the good parts. Pushing aside her worries in a vain attempt to quell her anxiety over the coming meeting, she finished the pig in two bites and washed its bits down with a few chugs of the barrel. Coasting along, she plugged the bung back in its hole and stowed away the empty barrel into her bag. There was a deposit on it, and she didn't want to litter, anyway.

Securing the flap and pulling in her wings, she plummeted through the clouds and careened around an outcropping on the adjacent cliff. Roaring with glee as she flung out her wings once more, she dodged another tall stone jutting out from the rocky face and ducked behind a long, leaf-covered tree branch blocking her way. Just because she had to fly out here and attend this meeting didn't mean that she couldn't have a little fun in the process. She deserved that for herself, at least, right?

Grinning from ear to ear, she sucked her wings in against her body and performed a tight spiral down toward the green field below. Wind whipping past her face, she reveled in the freedom of the moment and pushed all other thoughts of work, family, and other annoyances of her life from her mind. She had spent an entire lifetime sacrificing her own selfish goals and postponing her joy for the happiness and success of her family and co-workers. But now… they were all grown, moved on from her brood, or had abandoned her in their own personal quests for joy. Now it was her time.

That is, until this meeting was over. And then the next meeting. And the meeting after that. She had promised herself that after the divorce she would begin looking for new jobs, but that had yet to transpire. Whether it was a fear of the unknown, resistance to change, or just being a giant sucker to make others happy, she had spent the past two years continuing to work for this damn job which she had promised to quit so many times before. She loved the other dragons with whom she worked and it was one of the few real reasons keeping her there. Well, most of them. But the good ones, they were what made it worthwhile to wake up each morning and trek back into the office. Screw the salary. Screw the occasional use of the luxurious corporate caves around the world. Screw the annual bonus in gold coins if she met her quotas. None of those perks were worth her soul and its continued degradation.

Subconsciously scanning the ground below while working through her daily 'I hate my job and should quit' mental spiral, she saw the client's cavern off in the distance. Shaking her head in an effort to snap out of it, she dropped lower and billowed her wings to begin her descent. Slowing down from just the adjustment of her wing angle, she flapped a few hearty beats to bring herself to a low altitude and hovered just in front of the entrance to their headquarters. Two wingspans from the base of the mountain, she quit her flapping and gently alighted on the fine stonework leading to the main door.

Situated within the hollowed-out husk of a long-dead volcano, the headquarters of Bacchanalian Burritos was an impressive sight to behold. While not as glamorous as some of her other top-tier clients, it was hard to argue against the fact that their center of operations was pretty freakin' awesome. Located within a range of impressively tall mountains along the east coast of the United States, the dormant volcano which the entrance to the main cavern system was hidden was already a sight to behold. But once you knew where to look, one would be granted the opportunity to see that the real entrance was hidden behind a tastefully crafted waterfall. The foyer leading here featured an array of false entrances, literal smoke and mirrors, and according to rumors, a variety of deadly booby traps.

All this, she reminded herself, for a burrito company. The headquarters was the wet dream of every criminal master mind in the world who would love to hide away here and plot their next caper. From what she had heard, the only thing that it was missing was a fish tank in the middle housing a collection of sharks with head-mounted laser beams. The scene should have been played out in the climax of a spy movie, not a corporate meeting to discuss long-term investments and how to properly manage dividends.

But who was she to judge? She didn't have that money and never would. Besides, she didn't want to have a hollowed-out volcano where she could sit in her captain's swivel chair and steeple her fingers together while planning world domination. Her plan was to work as hard as possible while she could, save up a giant mound of gold coins, and then plan her escape. If she could find a nice piece of land on the shore of a calm lake, wrap her fingers around a hot cup of tea, and just drift off into old age to the sound of the birds and lapping waves against the beach, then she could die a happy dragon.

She didn't want power, per se; she just wanted to get herself on the right path to relax and enjoy her golden years in peace. In the meantime, though, she could still splurge and allow herself the opportunity to live vicariously through others of advanced means and suckle on the teats of their success. If she had to be working this weekend, she might as well enjoy it. And, if she could work toward tearing down the patriarchy when she could afford the time, then so be it.

That is, if her daughter could forgive her. She had missed her last hatching… and the one before that. So, she had promised, even resorting to an over-the-phone pinky-claw swear that she wouldn't miss this hatching. And of course, she had blown it. Walking toward the front desk to check in, she reminded herself to call Alicia as soon as she could to see how she was doing. Perhaps she could even pick up something fun for the whelps while she was up north in this part of the country.

Clipping the visitor badge clip to a scale on her chest, she took a seat in the lobby to await her escort. Seeing a mirror on the opposite wall, she fidgeted in her chair to get a better view and straightened her badge. Despite her years of service with the company and her exemplary record, Maggie still had to compete with the male dragons at the company on levels which they never had to worry about. The men could show up with dusty scales, wrinkled wings, and even, Tiamat forbid, bits of human meat stuck in their teeth, and nobody would blink an eye. Yet if a female dragon showed up to the office with even a tiny smudge of dirt on one of their claws, there would be a mass email sent out reminding all employees about appearance standards and representation of company values. It was told BS.

Taking a deep breath, she tried to think soothing thoughts and find her center within this anxiety-fueled torrent of emotions. She pictured playing with her grandwhelps, vacationing on the beach later this year, and sipping an iced coffee while reading a good book with sand between her claws. That's all that she wanted, really. Family, love, and the beach. Was that too much for a dragon to ask for?

Bringing her heartrate down to a more normal level, she opened her satchel and reviewed its contents. Printouts of the latest sales numbers for Bacchanalian Burritos, their current ad campaign imagery, and some boring paperwork which she needed them to sign while on this trip. She could have emailed it over, but it was nice to get the personal touch if she was going to be there anyway. Call her 'old school', but she liked the look of ink on paper, contrary to the young whelps in her office who wanted to do everything digitally these days.

Oh, and snacks. So many snacks. She couldn't go a few hours without needing to sink her teeth into something meaty, and if it had blood in it, all the better. Fried beef knuckles. Chocolate covered pig heads. Smoked deer legs with a dash of sea salt. Her mouth watered just thinking of it all.

"Mmmm" she said out loud without noticing. She was daydreaming about ripping the flesh from a deep-fried alligator when she caught the receptionist at the desk giving her the side-eye, for admittedly, good reason. If she had seen someone dream-scarfing a reptilian delicacy and having a full-body joygasm because of it, she'd think they were weird, too.

Composing herself, she straightened up in the chair and placed the satchel in her lap. She was about to go through the papers once more to memorize some of the key talking points to refine her presentation when the door to the lobby opened. Standing before her was a muscular dragon staring at her as if she were the only other dragon in the world. Quickly gazing from side-to-side, she realized that she kind of was, at least in this room.

"Magendron," he began, the words smoothly passing between his shining white teeth. Looking down at the tablet in his claws more carefully, he squinted before continuing. "Magendron, the Destroyer?"

Raising her wings, perhaps a little more quickly and perkily than normal, she rose from the seat and waved a claw his way. Starting towards him, Maggie tucked her wings behind her and moved through the array of empty chairs in the room.

"Magendron, here," she said, confidently. While she liked a dragon with a few more years of wear and tear in their scales, she wasn't going to waste the chance to check out a prime specimen of the next generation of the male gender. His pectoral muscles bulged beneath his scaley chest, outlined perfectly in his crisply ironed French cuff shirt. Strong, thick wings powered by well-toned bicep muscles protruded from his back, tucked behind and folded crisscross against his body. She noticed the younger males doing that posture lately as it was apparently all the rage in the larger cities. The gents of her era liked to drape theirs behind themselves vertically with the tips just hovering above the ground. While she was rather partial to the latter, she wasn't against adapting to new trends when they worked.

Granted, he probably still had flecks of his shell on his scales somewhere, but it didn't hurt to look. Besides, at her age, she wasn't exactly looking for anyone to warm her promethium glands up, if you catch the drift.

"But you can call me Maggie," she said, coyly. She hadn't intended on flirting with this male, but she had woken up on the wrong side of the cave this morning and decided to throw caution to the wind. Her mental faculties were currently preoccupied by thoughts of years wasted with her former broodmate, her kids not returning her messages, and this Tiamat-forsaken trip. She hadn't noticed it consciously, but it was as if she had shed her old, tired scales and emerged from the ashes of her dried out husk as a reborn dragon, casting aside her lifetime of self-sacrifice and repudiated dreams. Where there was once a shitty mood driving her to hate every moment of this pointless trip, there was now a renewed spirit of personal growth and a desire for happiness.

Smiling back, the scales on his face darkened ever so slightly as he processed her possible motives.

"Yes, ma'am," he replied. "I'm Walter, but most of my friends call me Watt. You can call me watt-ever you like, though."

His terrible pun elicited a grin and a girlish chuckle from Maggie. She typically hated puns, but it somehow sounded wonderfully silly coming out of his well-detailed mouth.

Watt motioned with his claw and extended his wing in kind to indicate the opened door. He was holding it with his tail, a tricky feat which had not gone unnoticed by Maggie in passing. It had been a while since a younger dragon had flirted back with her and she wasn't going to waste this moment, even if she had no intention of following through on her lustful shenanigans. It felt nice just to be considered.

"Thank you, Watt" she said, with a wink, her smile growing by almost a foot on each side.

Standing off to the right once she walked through the doorway, she allowed the younger male to pass by and lead the way to their next stop. Quickly looking up and down at his passing form, she took in the full scope of his toned, ripped body. If she had been a few decades younger and not showing the signs of so many eggs being laid, she'd push him off into a side cavern and have her way with him. Hell, she'd take flight and let him chase her to the clouds above, grappling her in midair, only to pin her to a nearby cliff to do as he pleased.

Her breath quickening, she was surprised to find her heart pounding in her chest. She felt the blood flowing through her veins, making its way down from her heart throughout her body, swelling in places where it hadn't gone in years. A glistening patch of sweat began to form on her brow, giving away her sudden oncoming arousal.

"What are you doing, Maggie" she whispered, quietly scolding herself. "Get it together!"

Placing a claw against the smooth stone wall beside her, she supported herself as a wave of light-headedness washed over her. She hadn't felt like this since her first century back when courting for a broodmate. Blinking her eyes and giving her massive skull a shake, she looked up to see the deep eyes of Watt staring back at her.

"Are you feeling unwell, Maggie?" Watt asked, the empathy oozing from his voice. It had been a long time since a male, a real male, cared about her well-being. The attention thrilled her.

"Yes, yes," she muttered through clenched teeth, trying to control the rush of air pumping in and out from her lungs. "Just feeling a little flush all of a sudden. Must have breathed too much fire this morning cooking my breakfast, that's all."

The look on his face screamed that he wasn't convinced, but he was too much of a gentledragon to push the subject any further. Not that she would complain about a little pushing from this hunk of draconian male.

Seeing her stand back straight and compose herself, he resumed walking with her in tow. He spent the next few minutes giving her a brief tour of the facility as they made their way through the labyrinth of caverns set into the mountain. It was very impressive and wowed her from start to finish. She couldn't believe that a food company which had just started a few years ago had already built up enough capital to afford such a location for their corporate headquarters. She was obviously in the wrong line of work.

Approaching a large stone and frosted-glass door, the pair came to a stop. Placing his clawed fingers upon the handle, Watt turned to look back at Maggie. His eyes, no longer smoldering with burning attraction, felt warm and comforting to Maggie.

"Have you met Grayson and Ansley before, Magendron?" he asked, care in his voice.

"No, not in person," she said.

"They can be, ah," he started, stammering in a way which she could tell from only her very brief time knowing the male, was completely uncharacteristic of him. "A bit much," he finally concluded, after what must have been a painful process of choosing the right words about his superiors at the company.

She knew the feeling. Much of her day was spent trying to remain professional and speak on her centuries of experience in the field, being honest enough with the client to steer them on the correct course, all while telling them that their shit didn't stink. It was a mentally draining task at times. What she wouldn't give to tell her clients how she really felt at times…

"I understand. Thank you, Watt," she said, putting a claw on his upper arm.

She could feel his scales bristle in excitement under her touch. Whether it was from embarrassment, excitement, or longing, she couldn't tell. But they calmed down almost immediately. He gently pulled back to break the connection, but as he moved, his bicep flexed, and the scales bulged beneath her delicate contact. A rush of blood surged through her, causing the already red tone of her facial scales to blush further. Retracting her claws as quickly as she had extended them, she put her hands together in an awkward clasp.

"This isn't my first rodeo, but I appreciate the warning."

He didn't look convinced, but he nodded in assent just the same and raised a bony knuckle to the glass. Giving it a quick rap, he waited until a word of acknowledgement emanated and put his hand upon the door handle.

"Here we go."

CHAPTER III

In her short time knowing Watt this morning, Maggie had made several assumptions about the strong, virile young male. One assumption that she had made was that he had perhaps exaggerated the concern in his warning about the two leaders of their company, Bacchanalian Burritos.

She had been wrong.

"Maggie!" they both bellowed as the door opened and she was led into the conference cave. Placing a clawed hand on the door opened by Watt, she jumped back in surprise and dropped her satchel as the two rushed towards her in excitement.

Grayson, the president and founder of Bacchanalian Burritos, roared into the air, belching fire at the low ceiling in the process. The outburst pushed the air from the room, filling the space momentarily with thick, acrid smoke. Even a hardy dragon such as Maggie, who was no stranger to dragonfire and the resultant ash which hung still in the cool mountain air, briefly coughed from the irritants entering her lungs.

Likewise, Ansley had leapt from her chair and dove towards Maggie as she had entered the chamber, wrapping her arms and then wings around the other in an intimate hug typically reserved only for family members and lovers. Ansley was neither of these to Maggie and had caught the other by surprise. Forcing a smile as she hugged the other female back, Maggie tried her best to slowly back away without seeming too obvious in her intentions. She looked over her shoulder to Watt for help, but he had already closed the door and disappeared. He had left her to fend for herself against these crazy dragons. While she wanted to be mad at him for that, she couldn't blame him and perhaps would have done likewise.

"Grayson! Ansley! It is so good to finally meet you in person," Maggie declared, trying to match their excitement level without seeming too sarcastic or disingenuous. Picking up her satchel and several discarded items from the floor, she looked inside the bag to see if anything was broken. Content with the state of things, at least in her satchel, she fully walked into the room and accepted her fate.

She couldn't fathom why they were so excited to see her after all these months in which they had remotely worked together on the upcoming project. After all, it was just to promote their new line of Alaskan moose-quarter tacos, it's not like they were unveiling an entirely new product. Granted, they were pretty good from what she had tasted in the samples mailed out to them in the early days of the partnership. They featured a whole hindquarter of an Alaskan moose, fur and bones removed, slow-charred on a spit with dragon fire, and garnished with select herbs and spices from around the region. It had done well in test groups with dragons from the northern states and western Canada, and they were all anxious to see it officially launch on the worldwide market. But why she had to fly out here for some hush-hush meeting with no advance information was still a mystery to her.

When they had finally calmed down from their oddly enthusiastic welcoming rituals, they stepped back and simply starred at her. After a painfully long moment, it was clear by the disappointed looks on their faces that they realized that she wasn't going to return their joyous introductions in kind. Grinning awkwardly as they mentally processed what should be done next, Ansley reached forward and offered her a chair, looking to Grayson for advice. His shoulders raised almost imperceptibly in what the Guinness Book of World Records would declare 'The Tiniest Shrug'.

Thanking them for the gesture while noting that she had apparently just made things super awkward, she took a seat and placed her satchel on the floor. Moving through her typical setup routine, she removed her computer, mouse, a notepad, and a pen. She was a diehard note taker and used the different media for different types of dictation, depending on if she needed to write, sketch a diagram, or create a model. Maggie prided herself on her professionalism and didn't waste any time getting to work. She already felt like she was starting a few steps behind where Ansley and Grayson would like her to be and she'd need to step it up a notch if she were to recover in their eyes.

Organizing her items for a moment and looking up when ready, she found the two of them watching her in eager anticipation. Grinning from horn to horn, they looked down at her setup confused and then chuckled a little.

"What's she doing?" Grayson whispered to the female at his side. Looking to the male out of the corner of her eye, she shooed him off and turned back to Maggie.

"Oh, you won't need any of that, silly!" Ansley said, smiling. "We have something so important to show you which cannot simply be captured in mere written notes. This requires your emotions, your passions, the culmination of your life's culinary experiences. In order to properly enjoy this moment, you will need to harken back to distant memories from your hatching onward and ponder the moments which led you to where you are today. Sit back, relax, and prepare yourself to have your tastes change forever!"

Ansley rushed off to the side of the cave where a cabinet sat against the smooth, stone wall. Maggie watched her with utter fascination. She was still equally confused and enthralled by the other dragon's introduction and didn't know if she should laugh or give her a standing ovation. Afterall, if they had her fly out here to attend this meeting in person on such short notice, it would obviously have to be the latter, right?

Thoughts of the wonderous potential possibilities battered the flood gates of Maggie's mind as she contemplated what could be hidden away behind the smoothly polished exterior of the small, human-made cabinet. Could they be unveiling some new secret ingredient and only she was to know? Could they be opening a new location in a big city and it would be her job to manage the financial transactions of the new entity? Were they acquiring another company and she'd be in charge of handling the stock purchases and merging them with the current portfolio?

The thoughts came to life and swirled around in her mind, sending her imagination into overdrive. It was as if they were tiny whelps themselves, caught on the breeze of lucrative ventures flowing through her mind's eye like warm rising air on a hot morning in the mountains. The rising currents buffeted their cute miniature wings, soaring them to the heavens and beyond.

"This could be my big break," she thought to herself. "This could be the account that I need to solidify my position within the firm and catapult my career on to bigger and better things. I could finally shed these boring go-nowhere accounts from my portfolio and be granted the privilege from on-high to tackle something meaningful. I can break the ever-present oppression of the glass cave ceiling at D-Trade and take my rightful place at the company."

She wasn't sure how long she had been staring off into the cool, dark tones of the cavern wall across the table from her, but when she came to, she found Grayson and Ainsley staring at her. Their perplexed facial features told her all that she needed to know, that she had been having another daydream. A dream, as usual, where she could potentially make anything close to her respective salary and possibly get on even terms with her male counterparts. They had been happening a lot as of late. Well, pretty much anytime that she had a bad meeting with her boss or one of the many malesplaining dragons on her floor.

"My apologies," she said, flushed. Taking a drink of water from the small barrel placed at her spot of the stone table, she quickly composed herself and returned her focus to the members of Bacchanalian Burritos. "Just a lot on my mind. But I'm here now! Tell me, what do you got? I'm dying to see it!"

She added as much sincere sounding enthusiasm to that last part as she could to help make up for her momentary brain fart. Ainsley's face lit up at the other female's excitement and jumped right back into her presentation. Standing to the side of a small wagon which had obviously been brought out while Maggie mentally teleported to a land where female dragons could be trusted with high level customer accounts, the female beamed with joy.

Granted, her gender had come a long way from the days where she would have been expected to simply tend to the cave and roast meat while her broodmate flew through the clouds and battled their foes, but it wasn't enough for Maggie. She wouldn't rest until she literally clawed her way to the top and melted the patriarchy down to its constituent elements in a white-hot bath of dragonfire.

Watching the other female, Maggie quivered in anticipation to see what was awaiting her eyes. The leadup had been enticing and she couldn't settle on which fantasy drummed up by her brain was sitting there under the moosehide covering. She stared in awe as two of Ainsley's claw-tipped fingers reached down to the center of the elegantly crafted sheet, gently pinching the leather, and paused, utterly teasing Maggie's imagination. She yearned to see what was hiding there beyond her vision. It could be her way out; her way to advance; her way forward to achieve all that she had desired after years of arduous work for uncaring male boss dragons. This was her time.

Time slowed down for Maggie. She could see the individual muscles gently flex under the scales on Ainsley's hand as she gripped the hide and began to lift it upward. The surface of the covering went taut and crease lines formed ridges and valleys propagating outward from her claws toward the edges of the hide. The passing material rode up and over the objects hidden below, continuing to tease Maggie's senses and hint at the wonderous delights sitting millimeters below, nearing their triumphant debut to the greater world. Maggie wasn't sure how long this process was going on for, only that she had no memory of blinking recently nor controlling the small pool of saliva building up among her knife-like teeth.

As Ainsley's claw continued its path toward the rocky ceiling above, the edges of the covering began to leave behind the hidden treasure below, exposing Maggie's desires like a melting glacier unveiling stones upon the New England countryside. Bit by bit, the obscured contents were revealed, and the colors and shapes bombarded Maggie's brain as it rapidly worked to stitch the images together. Her mind rushed to put it all together and take in the presentation before her. Looking through the gentle haze of dust kicked up by the leather covering yanked from the table on its journey to the other side of the room thanks to the muscular toss by the marketing VP, Magendron the Destroyer's psyche cracked, and she remembered why she had been given that name so many centuries ago.

CHAPTER IV

Wincing from the explosion of office supplies smashing against the opposite wall of the small conference cavern back at D-Trade, Maggie came to terms with the fact that she may have mishandled the situation back at Bacchanalian Burritos. While she had made her fair share of mistakes in the past, she was only dragon, after all, this one might have topped her long running collection of mishaps. Watching her boss run through one of his therapist-recommended breathing routines in an attempt to calm himself, she braced herself for the next round of outbursts.

"So, let's recap, shall we?" Argyle asked rhetorically, not even looking in Maggie's direction. "You know what? Hold on."

"Janice," the man spoke softly, yet sternly, into the speaker phone in the middle of the wooden table. "Could you please ask Kallan to join us, along with someone from HR? Thank you."

The shining, oiled surface of the ancient table was one of the hallmarks of the company. Built centuries ago by one of the original founders of the investment firm, it was the place to meet if something important needed to be discussed while at the D-Trade headquarters. Polished quarterly by the most skilled human carpenters on the continent, neither a scratch nor fingerprint was allowed to remain behind for very long before a tiny human from the custodial staffed was summoned to remedy the situation. The piece of furniture had seen the rise and fall of untold financial institutions yet stood as a landmark to the purity and trust embodied by the partners and general employees of the firm. For the most part, it was typically an honor to sit before it.

But not today. Not for Maggie. She continued to look down into the glasslike surface of the wooden table and wished that she were anywhere but there.

Hearing a crash of wood behind her, she looked up to see the door slam inward, the splintered remains of the once sturdy object hanging from its hinges, dangling precariously to the cavern floor. In the flurry of motion, she was just able to make out the visage of Kallan, the CEO of the firm, rocketing through the entryway. Maggie watched in horror as the slender female dragon alighted at the head of the table, trailed by an out of breath trio of lesser dragons travelling by foot and carrying stacks of folders and miscellaneous papers.

Maggie had a love / hate relationship with the woman. Well, not so much a relationship as a set of opinions and emotions founded through years of bitter give and take arguments with the woman, usually going in favor of the latter. It was her company after all, and Maggie was just a lower-level functionary keeping the cogs of industry spinning.

But the two females also had mutual respect for one another. Both had made the seemingly asinine decision to enter this male dominated field and had to start at the bottom of the bottom. If memory served her correctly, Maggie believed that Kallan had begun her career working in the mail room. The female spent years receiving stone tablets, rolls of leather parchment, and eventually, processing incoming electronic messaging once it had debuted. She had been here long enough to work through several phases of office technology, let alone the pile of countless male bodies she had to get rid of as she flew toward the upper echelon of the firm.

It was similar to Maggie's own personal experience, having started in the office supply department. She began her illustrious career during her final year of primary school and spent her time receiving supplies from the different vendors, organizing them in nice little rows on their shelves in one of the deepest, darkest caves within the complex, and then sat around and waited for dragons to need something. It was her duty as the youngest, and the only one in the department lacking the all-powerful male genitalia, to receive requests from the executives working in the upper levels and to process their needs. She'd gather up writing instruments, blank parchments and tablets, complicated and hurried lunch orders, and fly them up to the wood paneled caves at the top of the mountain.

The work, for the most part, was boring as hell. But on the occasional day, sometimes more often than she cared to recall, it could be absolutely disparaging. The male bosses at the time, thankfully none of whom were still employed, would treat the younger females like sex objects merely there to entertain their lustful desires. While she managed to escape without ever succumbing to the advances of many of her senior officers, she knew many other females who weren't as lucky. Many females would be threatened with termination if they didn't wear cute enough coverings, or if they didn't let the male dragons slap their tail in passing. Some even went further, doing whatever seemed necessary to keep their job and provide for their whelps back home.

She shuddered at the thought. It didn't occur to her at the time, but it may have been a blessing that she was significantly younger at the time, hated her job, and only saw it as a short-term opportunity to pad her resume and earn some gold coins for her hoard. She never worried about being fired because she had never planned on being there for longer than a few years between degree programs. But now, thirty-five long decades later, and she was still at it.

Slipping out of her melancholy state, she quickly sobered up and focused on the task at hand. You know, the task of being fired. It was important to look attentive while being canned. Watching Kallan settle herself in to a well upholstered chair slid into position behind her by one of the underlings, Maggie's stomach dropped down to the tip of her tail. Whatever sense of comradery she dreamt may have existed between the two females thanks to their many years on the front lines together had just burned up in promethium. The CEO's face had that look of a hunter ready to strike its prey, a visage which she had seen countless times in her own mirror whenever she needed to amp herself up to kick ass and take names. The eager burning in the eyes, the glint of teeth in the firelight, and the anxious tongue yearning for the taste of blood.

But now it was directed at her.

"Thank goodness, you're finally here," Argyle blurted out sarcastically. His words were dripping with malice and seething with half-bridled anger. "Did you hear what your little friend has been up to?"

Settling into her seat, Kallan slowly turned her head in the direction of Argyle and paused. When words would have flown out unfiltered from a dragon less in control of themselves, the composed CEO merely glanced her eyes upward at the standing male. Maggie couldn't see it from her angle, but the eyes were full of contempt for the uneducated swine.

"Little friend?" She asked, pronouncing the words slowly and with great deliberation. "Little friend. Magendron here is barely one of those two things. While smaller than an out-of-shape ouphe like yourself, she is rather strong and well composed for a female of her dragon type," Kallan said, sounding both like a compliment and insult.

Maggie wasn't sure if she were looking to insult her, Argyle, or both. If the latter, she had done so masterfully and efficiently.

"A friend on the other claw," she began, letting the sentence trail off after the word claw. She looked down at her own and appeared to be tending to a foreign object stuck to the claw. A piece of meat, dried blood, Maggie couldn't be sure. Flicking the detritus to the side, she returned her focus across the table. "Maybe perhaps in years long ago, but that status has been in flux and thrown into question over the past few days."

"You're damn right it's been thrown into flux!" Argyle bellowed, launching the seat backwards with his tail as he pushed himself away from the table. "What in the nine hells of Tiamat were you thinking out there?!"

"Argyle…" Kallan intoned, turning her head back to casually glance at the animated male.

"We gave you the easy assignment, Maggie. The

easiest! All you had to do was fly out there, try whatever their latest Tiamat-damned crap is that they're trying to peddle now, pretend that it tastes great, and then fly home. That's it! Do you even understand how simple that is? A freakin' whelp could have gone out there and done your stupid job."

"Argyle…"

"Well, not any old whelp, I assume," Argyle continued his rant. Sweat flooded his brow and saliva oozed from the corners of his toothy maw. "A male whelp, I suppose. Every time we send a female out to do a male's job, the whole thing goes to crap, and we look like idiots! Do you get that? Can your tiny little lady brain comprehend how much gold you just lost our firm?"

Argyle may not have seen the tail coming, but he certainly felt it. His body, though larger and more solidly built than the owner of the attacking appendage, flew a wing's span backwards and slammed into the stone wall. Thin cracks spider-webbed out from the point of impact and propagated beyond the outline of his crumpled form. Pausing in midair as his bulk continued to stick to the crumbling surface, he eventually slipped from the impact crater and fell forward. Laying prone on the floor of the cavern, Argyle grunted in pain, trying to get back to his feet unsuccessfully.

Kallan turned her head to Maggie and arched an eyebrow. "Are you alright, Argyle?" she asked without breaking eye contact with the other female. "You seem to have slipped and fell."

Through gritted teeth, the male pushed upward with both hands and the tips of his wings, raising his bulk from the floor and uneasily standing back to full height. A thin trickle of blood oozed from somewhere on his head, following a ridge in his scales to flow down between his eyes, down the side of his snout, and into his mouth. His tongue flicked out from behind his teeth to taste the iron-rich fluid, his eyes squinting ever so slightly as he restrained his fury.

"I'm okay," he started, clenching his fists. He took a step in Kallan's direction but was stopped short by a burst of smoke jetting from her nostrils. The look in her eyes signaled that more was to come if he didn't let this go. He got the message.

"Good," Kallan replied dryly. Turning back to Maggie, the hint of a smirk emerging upon her face, the CEO held her hand out to one of her assistants. A folder appeared and was gently placed in the female's waiting claws.

"Mistress Kallan, I can explai—," Maggie started anxiously, the words shaking through her teeth.

A jet of fire shot out from the right, Argyle's open mouth breathing hot air in its wake. "You better explain yourself," he shouted. "Do you realize how much you screwed—"

Kallan held up a single claw, stopping the male in his tracks and bringing all attention back to her. Perhaps Argyle was finally getting the point. Maggie sure knew that she did.

Slowly opening the folder, the female scanned the contents within and removed a single sheet. From what Maggie could see across the table, it appeared to be a printout of an email from Grayson at Bacchanalian Burritos. Maggie's blood boiled with the desire to dive into an explanation of her actions and to tell her side of the story before Grayson's could tarnish the narrative. She wanted to explain how she just wanted to be there for her brood and how she felt betrayed at the ridiculousness of the entire situation. But, if what just happened to that slug Argyle was any indicator, Kallan wasn't in the mood to hear any further interruptions. Besides, from what she knew of her boss, she had doubtlessly walked into this meeting already having made up her mind and was merely going through the motions for formality's sake. Whatever punishment was to be dished out to Maggie had already been decided.

"So, let's see," Kallan began, slowly. "It looks like you flew out to their site, as planned. Heavily flirted with an entry level employee… correction, an intern. Tsk tsk, Maggie," Kallan said, shaking her head.

It was hard to see in the gloom of the conference cavern, especially with the swirls of doom and anxiety flooding Maggie's brain, but she could have sworn that the other female gave her the tiniest of winks at that last part. She couldn't tell if Kallan was pissed at her, proud of her having crossed the line of professionalism for the potential grab at a little tail, or both.

"You then lacked any sign of enthusiasm at their presentation, sat glassy eyed through their entire discussion, rudely chewed them out over the subject matter of the meeting agenda, flipped their table over and sent it crashing into the wall, broken a presentation wagon, destroyed an antique cabinet, all before, and I quote 'burned the effing room to the ground' end quote" Kallan deadpanned, staring straight ahead at Maggie. "It says that you then fled the cavern and flew back here without checking out of the hotel and settling the bill. They had to cover your second payment, of which, we are now being invoiced with an outrageous markup."

Biting her lip, Maggie sat horrified in her chair. Everything which Kallan had just said was true, and even then, she had said the watered-down version which left out a lot of details. Did she do so because she didn't know, or was she trying to dilute Maggie's actions to help her save face in front of the other executives? Or was it to minimize what Argyle specifically knew just to stick it to him one more time.

Maggie pushed back in her chair and stood uneasily. Placing her hands on the tabletop, her claws left shallow scratches in the stone surface as she pulled her fingers inward into tight balls. She was clenching her clawed hands so tightly that thin trickles of blood oozed from each fist. Not aware of her own outward appearance, she also didn't see the swirling wisps of smoke escaping from her nostrils as she took a few deep breaths. "May I?" she asked through gritted teeth.

"Of course," Kallan replied, waving her claws palms-up before her in a sign of welcomed allowance. "But, from one girl to another, it would do you well to remember how your next few words may reflect on the reputation of your family within this community. It would be a shame to have any further unprofessionalism add to the disgrace which has already befallen your brood."

The comment smacked Maggie in the skull harder than any tail whip or claw slash that she'd received in a fight. She had rehearsed this in her head dozens of times since the morning of the incident. Her practiced speech had covered the entirety of the apology spectrum, ranging from complete subservience with no defense all the way up to attacking her bosses with dragonfire while ripping their promethium glands from their throats with her bare claws. But now... now there were more important things at play than she had considered just mere moments ago.

She wanted to tell her boss about her marital problems at home and how her recent divorce, the result of decades of neglect, sadness, and loneliness had been tearing at her insides for much of her recent memory. Her ability to trust any dragon moving forward was burnt to ash and blown away in the winds of regret.

She wanted to talk about how the lack of connectivity with her children and their own whelps drove a wedge through her heart, leaving her sad and alone, forgotten about by all but her closest friends. And even then, her friends had begun to fly south to warmer climates as they aged in their later years. For longer than she cared to admit she had remained in near isolation outside of the office, unsure of how to reintegrate herself in a society in which she once thrived. Much of her adult life had been focused on pleasing her broodmate, caring for her whelps, and maintaining a safe and clean cavern for them to live. Without that structure and routine, she found herself drifting aimlessly and unsure of what to do next.

She wanted to plead to the woman about how their mutually experienced struggles in a male dominated world had hardened them to the point of pure callousness, forcing her to often forgo any shared delight in the usual forms of happiness and frivolity enjoyed by other members of their species. A century ago, she would have squealed like a tiny whelp and gone wild with Ainsley. She would have enjoyed their stupid little meeting to savor in their new menu offerings, cheering with glee as the warm meat slid down her throat, roasting in the fiery heat of her digestive tract.

But she couldn't. Not any longer.

"You're right," Maggie said, conceding defeat. She wanted nothing more than to light up her second conference room in less than a week, but she couldn't bear the shame and guilt which would come of it. She had already tarnished her professional reputation and further actions could harm her personal one, as well. Few things were more important in dragon culture than family heritage. Despite her family leaving her behind as they moved onward, she didn't want to be the one carved into the tablets of history as casting a shadow on her lineage.

"I'm sorry," she continued. "I just couldn't bear one more thing threatening to drive a wedge between me and the happiness which I deserve. I couldn't handle one more ounce of responsibility for a non-value-added item on my to-do list. That morning with the clients, that... that meeting pushed me over the edge without a wing on which to hover. I missed the hatching of my grandchildren to fly out to Bacchanalian Burritos, on the premise of learning about a new product line up or other key business milestone which would propel the company forward, and in turn, my career."

She looked from one another to gauge their expressions. Argyle was seething with anger in the corner, and she wasn't sure if it was her or Kallan who was the bigger target of his wrath. The latter looked on with a stoic expression on her scales, not belying the true emotions simmering just beneath.

"I'm sorry, but I have given up years of my life for this company," Maggie explained, the pain pouring through her words, "And to miss meeting my new grandwhelps to hear Ainsley and Grayson go on and on about their goddamn new napkin colors to match the spice of the meat pushed me over the brink."

Looking at Kallan's face told Maggie that the other female didn't disagree and may have even been supportive in another time or place. Perhaps she would have even been sympathetic of her fiery outburst. But, with all that had been done, there was very little that she could do. Her claws were tied. This was far too public by now, having even appeared in some of the newspapers local to both D-Trade's and Bacchanalian Burritos' headquarters. What should have been an err in judgement was instead creeping into the spotlight of her overlapping social and professional circles.

"They were awfully excited about the rollout of their updated packaging to key markets in the next fiscal quarter," Kallan said, a chiding tone heavy on her voice. "Nevertheless, you know your place in this game. Smell the customer's shit, smile, and tell them that it doesn't stink. We support them financially, they sell their product, and we then reap our percentage of the rewards. Shit, smile, gold, that's all, Maggie."

"I know."

"I offer you this," Kallan began, holding up two claws. "One: you go on probation within the firm and have no customer contact for, I don't know, let's say, fifty years."

"Fifty years?! You've got to be kidding me!"

Kallan shot her a stern glance, quickly bringing the room back to silence.

"You will keep your job, but I don't want you anywhere near a customer meeting, correspondence, or any other avenue of communication where you could embarrass us, and yourself, once more until you learn your lesson."

"And the second?" Maggie inquired.

"And two," Kallan continued. "You pack up your belongings, quit, and we never speak of any of this again, for better or for worse. And you leave town. I don't want any of our clients to see you flying around here and remind them of any negativity pertaining to our venerated firm and its solid reputation within dragonkind."

Maggie, for the first time in her adult life, was absolutely dumbfounded. Usually ready with a quick witted response and able to roll with the punches, she had no clue what to say. She certainly didn't want to be on probation and receive such a long-term demotion in her career. The past centuries of hard work would be washed away in a wing flap. On the other hand, she couldn't just leave the company. She loved it here.

Right?

Wrapping her wings around herself, she quietly weighed the options in her head and tuned out the others around her. Kallan hadn't necessarily told Maggie to take her time and slowly consider her options, but she hadn't told her not to. What the heck was she supposed to do? She LOVED this job… well, she liked this job. She used to love it… centuries ago. But over the past few decades of watching her career plateau and everyone else move on without her had left her dissatisfied and craving more.

But more of what?

She needed to get out. Out of this room, out of this cavern system, and out of this town. Maggie had a large enough stash of gold back in her hoard that she could afford to kick back for a little bit and think about her next steps on the ever-evolving life plan. She had obviously bored her husband and her kids had outgrown her parenting services, so in the end, it really was all about her for once.

She knew what she had to do.

CHAPTER V

Pulling the wagon down the street toward her cave, Maggie finally began to cry. And not a 'thin trickle of salty residue trickling down her scales and drying in the late afternoon sun before they hit the ground' crying; but long, drawn out ugly crying.

She had remained strong throughout the meeting, despite that douche-nozzle Argyle trying to dragonsplain everything to her as usual. Of course, Kallan putting him in his place had helped a little. She had even remained composed while passing by her co-workers in the cavern on the way to her desk, packing her personal items up and loading them into this shitty old banker's wagon that they had given her for the deed. She had even kept herself together as she rode down the antique, rickety elevator from her midlevel office floor to the ground level far below and out into the lobby.

But once she had made it to the front door and was stopped by security to forfeit her badge, something broke inside of her. As she removed the small part of her identity which had been clasped to one of the scales on her chest for as long as she could remember, the floodgates opened. Hell, there was even a slight indent worn into the scale where she clipped it on every morning. Slamming the panic bar on the door and propping it open with her foot as she pulled on the handle of the wagon, she left the main cavern system of D-Trade for the last time and made her way out into the street.

She said that she wouldn't look back. But she did. The sight of the solid doors, now closed off to her forever, sent another torrent of tears flowing down her cheek. Turning away, Maggie pointed her wagon in the direction of her cave and trudged onward.

Kicking the door to her cave open an hour later, she flung the wagon through the entry way and slammed the portal behind her. Flicking the lock shut, she leaned against the door for a time, eventually sliding down until her tail hit the cold stone below.

Head in her hands, she contemplated her next move. She sat still like that for some period, not really aware of anything around her. At some point, the rumbling in her stomach forced her out of her stupor and set her body in motion. Just because her heart and mind weren't ready to move on, didn't mean that the rest of her body wasn't.

"Well, I should go visit the kids," she spoke out loud to the empty cave. She had discovered long ago that the silence of her personal cavern had great acoustics and that she was her own best listener. "I can finally meet the grandwhelps and check in on everyone. I mean, I have plenty of time now, right?" She laughed to herself, a sad tone edging its way into her voice.

She made her way over to the refrigerator and yanked upon the door. Removing a keg of Pinot Gris, she set it on the counter and reached up to grab an earthenware mug from the cabinet. Looking back and forth from the keg to the mug, she placed the mug back into the cabinet and yanked the cork out of the bunghole. Raising the keg to her mouth, she drained a healthy portion of the remaining fluid in one pull.

Setting the keg back down onto the counter, she pulled open the freezer drawer and removed a wooden crate from the bottom. Looking down inside with delight, she carried the crate and the now-lighter keg over the couch and plopped herself down. Removing one of the frozen chocolate-covered rabbits from the crate, she tossed it into the air and caught it with her teeth, swallowing it whole. She had found long ago that they were best when stored in the freezer as they kept her claws cleaner and added an extra little bite to the meaty filling. She tried not to eat them too often as she was trying her best to watch her figure, but they were just what she needed after days like today.

Leaning her head back against the couch, she wiped a tear from her face and closed her eyes. What was she to do? She had spent most of her life looking after others and caring for her brood. Or her company. Or her friends. Or any other dragon or thing on a list a tail's length long where she placed anything and everything above her own needs.

But not any longer. She needed something new; something for herself. But what?

Reaching over to the table next to the couch, she grabbed her laptop and hit the power button. She thought of updating her personal website to help pull in some prospective job offers while polishing her slightly out of date resume. She didn't completely abandon it over the years as she wasn't totally blind to the fact that she could be let go at any moment by those bastards over at D-Trade, but she had let it fall out of accuracy. Typing away at the keys to work on some wordsmithing needed to explain her recent roles at the firm, she saw the phone on the table next to her begin to vibrate across the smooth wooden surface before the ringer even began.

Scooping up the device with two claws, she looked at the screen to see that it was her best friend, Sparu. She wasn't really in the mood to talk to anyone right now, but if there was one dragon who she would make an exception for, it was Sparu.

After a lengthy update on her trip to Bacchanalian Burritos, this morning's meeting, and the complete emptying of the crate of rabbits, she took a deep breath and finally remembered to ask Sparu how she was doing and why she called.

"Oh, don't you worry about me, sweetie," the other dragon said, sympathetically. "You clearly needed to get that all off your scales and I wasn't about to slow you down. I was just calling to vent to you about one of my employees flying off the job this morning, but that's nothing compared to your day. The cavern floor is yours, dear."

"Wait a minute," Maggie said, her voice full of bewildered confusion. "You had one of your employees just up and leave in the middle of the day?"

"Yeah, weird, right? My handydragon decided that he didn't want to work on the cutest collection of cottages in the whole state of Maine and would rather go off and be a fisherdragon."

"But working for you is like every dragon's dream job," Maggie continued. "A cozy bed & breakfast on the coast of Maine. All the cute tiny little lobsters you can eat. Roasted dolphins. Deep fried sharks on the board walk. Ugh! I'm drooling just sitting here thinking about it."

"You should fly up here, then!" Sparu exclaimed. "You know that I always have a guest cave with your name on it."

"Oh, I wish," Maggie said, dismayed. "I'd fly up tomorrow morning if I didn't have to… if I didn't have to go to work tomorrow…" Her voice trailed off as she managed to finish the sentence and process her own words.

"That's right!" Sparu screamed through the phone, forcing Maggie to pull it away from her ear for fear of popping a drum. "You got canned, sister! You don't have anything going on tomorrow. Get your tail up here and we'll sort you right out."

CHAPTER VI

Just as the first rays of sunlight shone over the nearby mountain to illuminate her cavern, Maggie stepped out of the front door and into the cool morning air. Dragging a large leather bag behind her, she heaved it out of the way and locked the door. Gripping the round storm boulder in her rippled arms, she rolled the massive piece of stone into place and locked it in.

Flying up the face of the cliff to the next level of caves, she met her neighbor, Kotak, and exchanged a few quick pleasantries before handing over her keys. Maggie didn't know how long she would be up in Maine and had asked her most trusted neighbor to keep an eye on her cave in the meantime. She had recently watched Kotak's place and fed her pet humans while she had been away, so the other dragon owed her one. Especially for feeding those weird, scaleless pets of hers. Humans were disgusting.

Shivering at the thought of their weird little bodies with no tail or wings, she drifted back down to ground level. Gently stretching her wings, she pumped them hard a few times to help warm up the muscles and prepare for the long flight.

Gripping the leather straps in each hand, she swung the bag up onto her back and nestled it between her shoulder blades, just ahead of her wings. If she balanced it correctly, she'd barely feel it back there during the commute. Shimmying side to side and moving to and fro, she adjusted the luggage until it was just right and tightened the straps down hard.

Satisfied with her bag, she turned around and looked back on the door to her cave. She had spent so many wonderful years behind that stone. It was where she had first lived off on her own, fallen in love, laid the eggs which would go on to hatch her brood, and experienced all of the other important milestones in her long life. It was where her heart called home and would also stay there.

Sighing, she turned back toward the open air away from the cliffside and broke into a run. Flapping the giant leathery appendages, she felt the air underneath begin to build, traveling more quickly than the air above, providing her with that wonderful experience of lift and subsequent flight. Soaring out over the landscape which had provided the backdrop to everything seen from her kitchen window for so many years, she rose higher into the atmosphere until the features below were unrecognizable.

Pointing herself to the northeast, she rose into the low-lying cloud layer and rode the Gulfstream as quickly as it would allow. Fading into the background below, all traces of her former life fell out of focus, making way for new adventures.

CHAPTER VII

With the Sun reaching the apex of its flight path the next afternoon, Maggie slowly descended toward the cool, green dot just off the mainland coast. Loving the gentle, comforting caress of the rays of sunshine warming the top of her body as she raced through the chilly winds high in the atmosphere, she lazily made her way through the updrafts rising from the ground below. Heading toward the northern end of the island where the welcoming sandy outline of the shore awaited her, she swooped in low and brought herself in to gently alight on a grassy meadow just outside of the village proper. Though exhausted from the long flight, she instantly felt refreshed with a renewed vigor for life as soon as she landed safely on Mt. Desert Island.

Bouncing a few times as she patiently slowed herself down from cruising speed, she dropped to all fours and skidded to a halt before reaching the edge of the tree line. Feeling the moist dirt between her claws, she savored the experience with which she had missed for so long.

It had been decades since she'd visited Sparu at her place up in Maine and she regretted how much time had passed since her their last meeting. How many years had she sacrificed these simple pleasures of hers for the health and security of her family? How many times had she agreed to vacation elsewhere because her broodmate thought that Maine was 'too cold' or 'not exciting enough'? How many times had she skipped out on a vacation altogether because her boss needed her in the office working on some boring project?

But no more. Now was her time. Now, she'd selfishly spend her waking hours as she saw fit. Now, she would think about herself first and make others happy second.

The flight had been an easy one overall, taking Maggie from the outskirts of NYC over the Appalachian mountains and along the coast with the Atlantic. She loved the natural wonders of this trip and made sure to hit her favorites. The vast fields of grains tended by the humans to feed their cattle. The cool air rushing over the mountains, pummeling her with the intoxicating scent of freshwater creatures and rain. And the crashing waves of the ocean along the entire stretch from Massachusetts to New Hampshire, and on to Maine. She especially loved swooping along the beefy bicep arm of Cape Cod as she swung around and launched herself northward on the final leg of the journey.

Not wanting to burn herself out, she had stopped late last night in the White Mountains of New Hampshire to rest her wings and recharge her batteries. She had always been fascinated by the area given the rumors that the current line of dragons had originated in the region. Aside from the quick stop, however, and of course a few short breaks for hunting meat along the way, she had flown continuously from her door to Sparu's.

Dropping the bag from her back, she flopped over sideways and sprawled out on the ground. Settling in, she rolled around in the grass to stretch her aching muscles and work out a few kinks in her wing joints. She reveled in the feeling of the chlorophyll from the thousands of tiny blades of grass rubbing into her well-worn scales and filling their voids with the life sustaining green liquid.

She didn't need to sleep per se, but she definitely needed to take the weight of her skull from her neck for just a tiny bit. Resting her head on a soft-looking bush, she had laid there for all of five minutes when she decided that her eyes did indeed need resting and that she wasn't exactly in a rush to go anywhere. Curling into a ball, she was soon fast asleep in one of the most well-deserved naps of her life.

A short while later, unsure of how much time had passed, Maggie awoke with a start when her subconscious mind noticed a distinct reduction in light shining upon her face. Waking herself with a jolt, she instinctively pushed backward through the grass with her hindlegs and stared up into the late afternoon Sun. Aside from a blueish hue, she couldn't make out who or what it was due to the intruder strategically placing themselves in an eclipsing position to Maggie's eyes. So, she did what any half-asleep dragon would do when woken from their slumber prematurely by an unknown agent: she swept the legs with her tail and belched a warning shot of dragonfire.

Seeing the source of the shadow go down in a heap, she shot backwards and leapt to her feet, readying her body to defend herself at all costs. Rubbing the sleep-induced grogginess from her eyes, she held out one claw in front of her chest while cleaning her eyes with the other.

Scanning the tall grass for the spot where the shadow demon, or whatever monstrosity had tried to attack her, fell and took cover, she quickly found a depression in the vegetation. Slowly working her way around the depression in a spiral approach, she inched herself closer and closer to the unseen target with each progressive step. Working her way toward the edge of the crushed grassed, she pulled her arm back in preparation for the killing strike. Flexing her claws, she adjusted her footing in the dirt below and braced herself for the next move. This was a kill or be killed situation, she realized, and she wasn't about to back down from a fight. It had been a long time since she had fought another being of this size and stature out in the wild, but it didn't mean that she had forgotten how.

Tensing the rippling muscles of her arm, she raised her claw in anticipation of the swing and readied herself for her next attack. The waiting was what she hated the most. If only this damn thing would leap out from the grass and fight her like a true warrior. Quickly scanning side to side, she took in every blade of grass, every insect, every shimmer of the leaves on the trees fluttering in the cool afternoon breeze. Nothing would get past her senses.

Slowing her breathing and focusing her mind on the moment, she flicked out her claws on her other hand, ready to strike with either or both as needed. Stepping forward through the low vegetation, she brought herself to where she last saw the being go down, while also stepping to the right a little each time. She wanted to circle the position just a bit to throw off the creature and its anticipated counterattack. Walking along, she approached a dried tree branch laying in the grass below her line of sight. She never saw it, even as her foot came down upon it.

Crunch.

The grass in front of her began to flutter back and forth and a low groan emanated from the spot in the middle of the depression. Breaking into a run, Maggie leapt into the air, aiming her deadly claws and teeth at whatever lay hidden below.

"Maggie, no!" a familiar voice shouted from below her. Maggie shot out her wings and pumped them vigorously, launching herself upward and away from the source of the sound. Recognizing the voice, she immediately blushed with embarrassment and circled around to land next to the spot.

Feet back on the ground, she walked over to the high grass and reached a claw down to help her old friend up.

"What is your problem, you ole tosser?" Sparu groaned out as she was helped to her feet. Brushing dirt and bits of grass from her light blue scales, she stood straight and cracked her back. "I came out to see if you had arrived yet and found you goofing off in the field taking a wee nap. Now you're attacking your oldest friend for simply waking you up. Are you not batting on a full wicket? Have you completely lost the plot?"

Laughing, Maggie instantly remembered why she loved this dragon so much. "Oh, Sparu! How I have missed you."

"Apparently not with your tail!" the other female retorted. "That was a mean sweep back there, lass. Have you been working out? And what kind of way is that to greet someone? Next time I'll just leave you there in the grass to get nibbled on by the mice and the ants. See how pretty your little scales look then."

The other woman scowled at Maggie and crossed her arms in annoyance as she waited for the incoming reply. Maggie gave her none and leapt forward, slamming into her, and wrapping her friend in a warm hug of both arms and wings. It had been years since she had seen Sparu, and even then, it was for short breaks when work and family time permitted. This was the first time in as long as she could remember since they were whelps where she could just relax and enjoy her time with her oldest, dearest friend.

Walking back to town a short while later, the two females were deep in conversation trying to catch up on lost time. They had decided to walk rather than flying to better talk without the sound of rustling air confusing their words. They were in no rush and had all the time in the world. Well, not all the time, as Sparu still had her job after all, which was the original intent for this trip.

"So, what do you think?" Sparu asked, after explaining the details of the job and the current status of her campgrounds.

Maggie had been uncharacteristically silent for a few minutes after her friend had concluded her sales pitch for the position. A few days ago, she would have laughed at the prospect. She had been a well-paid employee of one of the largest investing firms in the country. Maggie could have had her pick of the egg clutch of any job that she wanted in her field and wrote her own paycheck.

But then she threw that all away in the blink of an eye. Looking back, she had thought long and hard during her flight to Maine that perhaps she had self-sabotaged herself. Maybe she wanted to quit and leave that life behind but was too afraid to make the judgement call on her own. Maybe she needed to force some other dragon into making the decision for her.

What she needed now, though, was a reset on her life and a fresh start somewhere new. Breathing in the cool, salty air blowing over the harbor, she realized that this place was about as fresh as it got. She would be an idiot for passing this up.

Turning to her friend, she smiled, shooting out a small gout of flame between her razor-sharp teeth. "Let's do it."

CHAPTER VIII

Opening her eyes as the first golden rays of sunshine penetrated the gently billowing curtains on the window, a slow grin spread across Maggie's face, replacing her feeling of confusion as she remembered where she was. Pulling the warm, woolen blanket up to cover her chin, she looked around the simple, yet comforting room. It was cool and crisp thanks to the cold night sharing its frigid breeze through the one-inch gap she left in the window. She loved being cold and heaping blankets over her body while she slept. You could also get warm if cold by adding more layers, but not as easily cool when it was warm. She'd never understand her weird kin who enjoyed living closer to the planet's equator where it was constantly hot and sticky with humidity and sweat.

Stretching her legs, arms, wings, and tail out away from her core, she must have looked like a giant, draconic starfish from above. Feeling several bones pop in and out of position, she cracked her long neck satisfyingly, finally feeling right in her body. She didn't know how long she had slept, but it must have been the deepest slumber she had had in as long as she could remember.

Rolling over, she found the small mechanical clock on the nightstand. It was an older model, showing light oxidation from the salty sea air, but added to the simplistic comfort of the room. It was unassuming, non-threatening, and reminded her that it was important to know the time to get her tasks done for the day, but without the in-your-face pressure to wake up early to do it. Reaching over with her claw, she turned the item until she could see the face and gasped.

"Nine o'clock!" she proclaimed to the empty room, jumping from the bed. "I can't believe that I slept that late," she scolded herself. "I'm going to be late for... for... nothing. Absolutely nothing."

For the first time in as long as she could recall, she had literally nothing to do. She didn't need to get ready for work. She didn't need to get the kids off to the academy. She didn't even need to clean up after that lazy, filthy broodmate of hers. She only needed to take care of one dragon from now on, and that was her.

Letting off a small gout of victory dragonfire, she leapt from the edge of the bed and landed gently on the stone floor of her cave. She had barely had the chance to look around last night after getting settled in due to her sheer exhaustion. But now that she had the opportunity, she had to admit that Sparu had done quite well for herself.

"This place is so freaking cute!" she said to the empty room.

"Why thank you," a voice called out from the now open doorway.

Startled, Maggie whipped around, her tail slashing at the portal to the room.

"Will you quit that crap!" Sparu shouted at her, ducking the attack while struggling to maintain balance of the tray full of food in her claws. The steaming cauldron of tea tipped back and forth on the tray, spilling some of the light green fluid. Shooting her neck down in a blur, she caught the sides of the cauldron between her teeth and stabilized it.

"Oh, dear!" Maggie yelped, lunging forward to help Sparu with the tray of food. "I am so sorry! I didn't hear you come in."

"Well, I just came by to see if you were awake yet and treat you to a hearty breakfast for your first day on the job," Sparu replied, carefully dropping the heavy tray to the small table in the corner of the room. "What I hadn't planned on was being viciously attacked by a googly eyed tourist on my own property."

Maggie laughed. She had definitely been enamored with the place and had been completely lost in her daydreams.

"I'm sorry for sleeping in so late… boss."

That made Sparu bellow with laughter. "For starters, don't call me boss. We go back way too far for those kinds of formalities," she continued. "And secondly, you'll find that if it doesn't involve food, things are pretty laid back around here. We keep the food piping hot and ready before the visitors wake up for the day, but everything else is on vacation time. As long as you keep things in working order, you'll be just fine."

"Well, that doesn't sound so hard!" Maggie exclaimed, excitedly.

"Things tend to fluctuate in difficulty, depending on how well you stay up to speed on maintenance and how hard the hooligans are on the toilets," Sparu said. Everything else is pretty easy going.

"Where should I begin?" Maggie garbled, trying to talk through a mouth full of food. "Ugh! This is so good. Are these fresh blueberries?"

"You know it, hun," Sparu replied, smiling a big toothy grin from horn to horn. "Just picked a few bushels yesterday afternoon and cooked them up this morning in our pancakes and waffles. I've even got some pies in the oven that'll be ready for later."

"I forgot how much I missed it up here."

"Well, we'll see how much you still like it after working through this list," Sparu said as she handed a piece of paper to the still chewing Maggie. "Finish up that plate of deliciousness and go find Seamus when you're done. He'll help you get started."

Wide eyed, Maggie scanned the long list and visibly gulped, despite having already swallowed her food. "That's a lot of tasks," she said, trailing off.

"You don't need to do them all today," Sparu reassured her, picking up one of the steaming kegs from the table. "That's just the current to-do list in descending order of importance. Start at the top and work your way down over the next few days. And if any hot jobs come up, I'll keep you posted."

"Okay," Maggie muttered, still reading. "Who is Seamus and how do I find him?"

"Seamus is the local lighthouse keeper, but he's a jack of all trades in our community," Sparu explained, gently blowing on the keg of green tea to cool it down. She tested it and took a careful sip. "I asked him to pick up the slack until you arrived to fill the position."

"It's been a while since I had someone fill my position," Maggie said under her breath.

Sparu spit out the tea she had just sipped, spraying some in Maggie's face.

"Ugh!"

"Oh, ha ha," Sparu spurted out, more tea flying. "I'm sorry, that is kind of gross. But it was your fault. And to answer your unspoken questions, Seamus is not single, but yes, he is handsome as hell."

An hour later, Maggie was walking through the hodgepodge of small bungalows and vacation caves dotting the premises. Looking around the premises, she couldn't believe how much the place had grown since she last visited many years ago. Granted, a lot had happened in the meantime, so perhaps her memory was a little fuzzy, but she didn't remember it being so charming and quaint while also being simply massive.

While the Drag Inn bed & breakfast had initially started out as a small cavern system dug into the side of a rocky hillside on the island, it had grown substantially over the years by the succession of laborious owners. The founding owners had been a broodpair looking to rent out extra chambers in their home cavern. Over the years, the bonded couple had hollowed out additional rooms within their personal cavern system, blocked off their own area, and dug out hallways connecting the system within the hillside. This was then continued by the next owner, his family, and likewise for the next century by the descendants of that family.

Every decade or so, another set of rooms would be added down a newly dug hallway. When times were good, the owners even added in recreational facilities, such as the swimming pool, gym, and some multipurpose rooms adapted for general use. Each time something was needed and the time and labor were available, the system evolved organically to suit the new needs.

Under Sparu's ownership, a dozen gigantic boulders were rolled down from the top of the mountain and arrayed around the primary cave in previously unkempt fields. Sparu had taken chunks of rubble from the hill above, rolled them into an eye-sore of a field and created luxury accommodations. Each boulder had been hollowed out, given flame-carved doors, windows, and running water, and was opened up to any weary dragon finding themselves wandering through the area. They became so popular that she then added them as bookable rooms for the inn and started charging money for tourists.

If there was one thing to accuse Sparu of, it was acting too conservatively. She owned land all over the island but declined to capitalize on it. A life-long nature lover, she had the zoning board change most of her property to dedicated green spaces so that nothing could ever be developed upon them.

She then designed walking trails leading from her inn to all the best places around Mt. Desert Island. Some even went as far southwest to connect with the trail system within Acadia National Park. Thoughtfully located benches were placed at key points of interest and beautiful vistas, with seating for both dragons and humans alike. Some might laugh and wonder why a dragon would hike or why she'd want to cater to the tiny little scaleless denizens, but Sparu felt that the wilderness should be enjoyed by all and wanted to do her part to contribute.

On cooler days, she would sometimes walk around

with a wagon full of steaming tea and pass out kegs and tinier mugs to thirsty visitors, whether they were her paying customers or not. During the apple season, she would buy apple juice from the human farmers and brew a delicious vat of mulled hot cider with tiny little sticks of cinnamon floating around in the keg. She was even known to bake tasty pastries and leave them out on a table in the main office for all to enjoy.

It was stories like these which had pulled at Maggie's heart strings over the centuries, luring her to the vast wilderness that was the state of Maine. Sparu had tempted her on multiple occasions to get her wings up there and have a girl's weekend, but Maggie had always found an excuse to not go. There was always work, or a kid's sports game, or something with which her broodmate needed help. There was always a thing or a commitment to some other dragon's happiness that Maggie found a way to stop herself from having a little fun.

But no more. Now it was all about her.

Lost in her reverie, Maggie had barely kept track of where she had been walking. Circling the collection of bungalows, she had come across a trail that looped through the inn's property and had absentmindedly taken the path. Walking along admiring the scenery, she had barely acknowledged the sound in the distance, but it was one which brought her great comfort and harkened back to simpler times.

Chop. Chop. Chop.

Someone was nearby chopping wood and based on the rhythm and ferocity of the strikes, Maggie guessed that it was a dragon. And a strong one, at that. She couldn't remember the last time which she had heard that primitive and oddly-relaxing staccato of dragon and steel working together in harmony to accomplish a task. It was not a sound which you would have heard back in her home as they used a dragonfire-lit gas system, but years of absence wouldn't allow her brain to forget this memory. A wave of nostalgia washed over her as memories of her father chopping wood on overnight camping trips rushed into the foreground of her thoughts.

Round the bend in the trail, she passed a large copse of trees and found a male dragon standing there with his back to her. He was in the process of raising an axe above his horns, arms as thick as tree trunks gripping the handle tightly in his claws. She watched as the scales on his biceps rippled with excitement as they were tasked with lifting the heavy tool in preparation for the subsequent chop.

The dragon's arms flexed as he brought the head of the axe up and past his head, then sliced through the air in a blur, diving into the top of the log deftly balanced on a well-worn tree stump below. The hardened, razor-sharp edge of the axe penetrated the wood deeply, driving through the center of the log until it found what it was looking for. Forcing its way through the fibers of the target, the log offered no resistance and submitted its will to the whims of the blade. The two halves of the log, like a long pair of cream-colored legs, opened and separated for the tool to go to work.

Breathing heavily, Maggie reached up to her chin to find a thin trickle of blood running down her scales from her lip. Feeling around with a claw, she found that she had apparently bit her lip in the moment, watching this stranger go to town on that pile of logs. Feeling faint, she reached out for one of the trees nearby and steadied herself. The tree shook under the force of Maggie's now-stabilized body, rattling the branches and leaves above their heads.

Hearing the rustle of the branches above, the dragon stopped mid-stroke and turned around, looking straight at Maggie. Unable to breathe, she froze against the bark of the tree as she took in the sight of the male.

Tilting his head down to see her, his dark eyes bore into hers. She tried to look away, but they were drawn back, as if the sum of the Earth's magnetic field originated deep within him, pulling her gaze in to his and only his. The corners of his mouth turned upward in a gentle smile as he took in her sight. He moved closer to her, the late morning sunlight shimmering off his worn, maroon scales. Not roughed up as if he had been a pit fighter with the outer layers of his scales scuffed off, but more worn smooth like a tiny pebble trapped in the eddy current of a fast moving river. She wondered what he could have done all these years to get his body to look like that. She'd yearned to find out.

Breaking free from his tractor beam like eyes, she looked away and noticed that he had reached out with his hand. Staring down at his outstretched claw, Maggie couldn't fathom what his intentions were. Was he reaching out to her, begging her to relinquish her body to him and satisfy all of his draconian delights? Or was he simply trying to shake her hand, something which few males ever did for a female. Or did he view her as a threat, sneaking up on him in the woods while his back was turned, ready to strike? Was he about to strike first and eliminate the threat? Tiamat, she wished it were the first one.

"Good morning. Are you Magendron?"

Maggie stared back at him in silence. She couldn't

move. She begged her body to react, to wake up, to escape from its self-imposed prison, but it would not—could not. Her loins were on fire, blood rushing from throughout her body to engorge her tissues in preparation for acts which she was ashamed to admit. It had been so long since another male paid any attention to her, and she found herself jumping violently towards her own hastily drawn conclusions.

Was she really this horny that she'd lose it every time a guy looked at her in a non-offensive manner? Had she spent too long around the likes of Argyle and her broodmate to appreciate a normal male simply wanting her company, or to just converse? How messed up was she and when would this end?

Maggie saw his lips move again but heard nothing. Get a grip, Maggie.

"Pardon me," Maggie managed, though unsure where this courage finally found itself. "I didn't catch that. What did you say?"

Chuckling, the male leaned back and took her in. "Are you Magendron? The new handymale?"

She stared at him, unsure how to even begin a real conversation.

"My apologies," he said. "I mean, handy*dragon*. Sparu mentioned that one of her friends was coming in yesterday to fill the position."

"Yes, I was coming," she answered, shaking her head at the absurdity of the wording. "I mean, I came. I came yesterday. I came to fill the position."

The male stuck his claw out again after having been left hanging the first time. "Scorcher's the name. But my friends call me Seamus."

"Maggie," she replied in kind. "You can call me Maggie, or anything that you like."

Chuckling again, he looked down at her. He stood a full wing's width above her, so he spent much of their short conversation looking down. She absolutely adored it. Maggie loved a taller dragon, which when she thought about it, should have been the first red flag about her former lover. The dragon had stood slightly shorter than her and she had often found it to be embarrassing to fly down the streets with him. She told him that it hadn't bothered her, but deep down inside, it always had.

"Well, Anything-That-You-Like, why don't you grab some wood," he said.

"Excuse me," she retorted, both flustered and a little annoyed. Just because she was dreaming of him having his way with her doesn't mean that she actually wanted him to be so pushy. It was kind of hot, but seriously though, slow down. It's a marathon, not a sprint.

"The wood," Seamus said, pointing his tail toward the mound of chopped firewood that he had obviously spent the morning preparing. "I've had enough chopping for the day, so we might as well load up the wagon with the wood and carry it around to the bungalows. I will chop more later and bring a load to the main cavern system after lunch."

Green face turning a shade of red as she blushed, she couldn't believe what she thought that she had heard him say. "Yes, the wood… great idea."

Together, the two dragons quickly stacked the perfectly chopped logs into tight rows of piles on the massive wooden wagon. Balancing the pile just right, Seamus quickly secured the bundle with a few quick passes of thick rope, neatly working a knot in the middle to hold it all together. She marveled at how rapidly he manipulated the cord and tied the knot deftly with the tips of his claws and quick turns of his wrists. She wondered what else he could tie up like that.

Gripping the thicken wooden handle at the front, the two dragons pulled the wagon down the path and distributed the wood throughout the grounds. They left tidy piles of firewood outside each bungalow as they made their way through the trail system, moving more quickly and easily as the wagon lost weight along their trip. Maggie relished the chore, despite having to trudge along the dirt paths pulling the wagon wheels over exposed roots and rough rocks.

She loved being side by side with the newcomer. At times, their wing tips would lightly graze against each other as they worked their bodies through the task. The gentle touch of his wing on hers sent shivers of excitement through her veins. She couldn't remember the last time that she had felt this purely exhilarated over something so simple as stacking firewood. Maggie hated to admit it, but she felt like a youngling all over again, falling in love for the first time.

Nearing the end of their circuit and thankfully dragging an almost empty wagon, Seamus offered to pull the handle by himself and let Maggie walk unencumbered. Kindly taking him up on his offer, she spent a few moments looking around at the trees, flowers, and tiny wildlife living around the inn. It was a vibrant ecosystem with a cacophony of sound, telling all who would listen about the wonderous collection of life thriving all around them.

Smiling, she looked over to Seamus to see if he was

enjoying the moment as much as she was. However, he was just staring ahead, blank faced as he trudged along the path. She wondered if he was just some big, strong, dumb brute who only focused on building his physique and wouldn't care less about the natural world around him.

"This place is beautiful," Maggie prompted, hoping to draw him out of his silence. "Have you been here long."

He didn't answer but continued pulling along.

"Seamus," she tried again. "Have you been here in Bar Harbor long?"

When he didn't answer the second time, she cautiously reached back for the handle, allowing her claws to lightly graze his on the wooden shaft next to hers. The contact, a connection back to the physical world from wherever his mind had been, brought him back instantly. He looked down to see their claws touching, and quickly adjusted his grip several inches away.

"You okay in there?" Maggie inquired. She was concerned about his well-being, but also a little curious as to what could distract the male so deeply that he would ignore a pretty dragon such as herself trying to talk with him.

"Yes, my apologies," the male said to her, briefly making eye contact but then quickly turning back to the road ahead of them. "It's just been a while since I've spent time with a dragon, like… like you. Just had me thinking."

Not knowing what to say, she turned back to the path ahead of them, as well, watching the scenery for a moment as she contemplated her next words. Walking along, she looked back to his left claw clenched tightly on the well-worn wooden handle. Trying her best not to stare at the muscular digits and imagining what he could do with them, she craned her neck ever so slightly to get the proper vantage point. Sure as heck, there it was.

A wedding band.

Turning forward, she found herself, once again, completely without words and unable to form the simplest of sentences. He was married but hadn't been with a female dragon in a while... maybe she had moved away for work? Maybe it was a long-distance relationship? It was weird for any species, but not as hard for dragons as they could fly for almost free whenever they felt like it.

Looking to break the awkward silence, especially considering that she really did want to get to know the male, she redirected her attention and set her mind back on track.

"So, Seamus, do you and your wife live here on the island?" Maggie inquired, trying her darnedest to probe the wife-situation without sounding too desperate. "What do you both do when you're not hanging out with Sparu and her idyllic estate?"

"My wife—" Seamus began, stumbling over the two short words. Maggie wasn't a speech pathologist, but even she knew that he could pronounce the words correctly had he wanted to. Or without being loaded by external pressure. This went deep, and Maggie was about to go as deep as needed. "My wife and I live just off the shore from here, due northwest. Are you familiar with the Crabtree Ledge Light?"

"No, what it is?"

"It's a lighthouse out in the middle of the water," Seamus explained. "The humans call it a sparkplug design as that's what it looks like compared to some part in one of their little vehicles. Well, the wee creatures built it a long time ago to help alert their sailors to the shallow waters and nearby shorelines to stave off shipwrecks. After they abandoned it before their big war, us dragons took it over after our rise to prominence."

"Thanks be to Tiamat," Maggie stated involuntarily. The phrase had been ground into her since her youth when they learned the draconic history in school to the point where uttering the words had become automatic. The mighty dragon goddess Tiamat had brought the dragons out of seclusion and taught them to resist and overpower the tiny, yet clever and sneaky humans. Once the smaller beings were decimated in vast quantities and reduced to miniscule scatterings of the weakest remainders of their species, the leader of their kind swiftly moved into position and took control of the world.

"Thanks be to Tiamat," Seamus replied in kind.

"Anyway, my grandfather was the first dragon to take on the job of lighthouse keeper. He repaired the tiny dwelling after it had fallen into disrepair by the lazy little beings, and eventually expanded upon it to provide for our larger bodies," he continued.

Maggie could hear the honored pride underlying Seamus' voice. He was clearly a lighthouse keeper through and through. Maggie wished that she could have a job someday where she felt that magnitude of pride and personal satisfaction with her work.

"During my father's time," Seamus said, "the family razed the water-beaten dwelling down to the underwater foundation and rebuilt it upward. The tower was widened to accept our body size and elevated over one hundred feet into the air. The new tower dwarfed the existing structure, allowing for more dragons to stay onsite, more comfortable working conditions, as well as better visibility range with the dragonfire lantern.

"From a young age just after hatching, my father and mother trained me in the skills needed to properly maintain the lighthouse. I began taking their shifts after primary school and have been running the tower by myself since they retired."

Maggie listened intently to the dragon's every word. She couldn't recall the last time that she had met another dragon as interesting as this male and didn't intend on letting the conversation end any time soon. She hadn't planned on coming up to make many friends beyond Sparu so quickly, but she liked this one—a lot.

"I'm confused, though," she said, trying not to sound too embarrassed. "Why would dragons need a lighthouse? We can fly everywhere that we need to go and can easily see the difference between land and sea in the infrared spectrum. Not to sound insensitive, but why would dragonkind even need a lighthouse?"

The look of shock on Seamus' face forced Maggie to recoil ever so slightly. She thought that he was mad at her, but a quick moment later revealed that he was being sarcastic.

"Ooh!" He groaned, clutching his chest with his free clawed hand. "The pain! It is too much for me to bear! Please, will some dragon call a doctor, I need someone to finish tearing out my heart."

Maggie looked back at him, cocking her head to the side. She didn't want to laugh at his lame joke, but she could feel the smirk forming across her mouth involuntarily.

"Har har har," she continued. "I'm sorry! I'm not

trying to sound like a jerk. I am legitimately curious. I have spent most of my life in the Midwest and New York with very little time on the water itself. The concept of a lighthouse is unknown to me. I get why the humans might need them, but why would we?"

"Well, after the Great Rise," Seamus began, "many of our kind wanted to completely wipe out the humans. I wasn't one of them, but I couldn't disagree with the rationale exhibited by those who felt that way. They had heard stories passed down through their families, and some had directly witnessed the horrors wrought by the humans themselves. They wanted revenge and they were going to have it one way or the other. They wanted retribution for the thousands of years of torment and slaughter which we suffered at their tiny little hands."

"I remember the stories," Maggie added. "I grew up after the Great Rise and have always known the humans to be a small minority in our lands. It's hard to imagine that they could pose such a threat."

"Not on their own and in such small numbers, they can't," Seamus replied. "But I remember a time when they had sufficient numbers, tools, and their blasted weapons to pose that threat. I am happy that they are not in power anymore."

"But…" Maggie contributed, sensing the change in verbal tack.

"But," Seamus continued, chuckling at her anticipation of his words and admitted accuracy. "But I have accepted their presence and eventually learned to live side by side with them. Well, at least some of them.

"When they want to be, humans can be very productive, creative, and are great at problem solving. They also have smaller hands and delicate tools capable of working with tiny pieces of equipment and materials which we couldn't dream of manipulating. That's why some of us on the coast adapted to fishing from the sea many years ago. Not only can we catch more fish in our larger and heavier nets than the humans can, but we can also catch whales, sea lions, and other large seafaring denizens which are more palatable to our tongues."

"So, what do you do with these wee little fish that you catch, trade them with the humans?" Maggie asked in bewilderment.

"Yes, actually," Seamus answered. "It's quite profitable for both parties. They provide us with service and repair to many of their antiquated systems for electrical production and Internet maintenance. These tasks are often beyond our physical capabilities and above the mental faculties of some of our less-than-academic brethren. We, in turn, provide them with food, heavy lifting in some of their projects, and protect them from the occasional predator haunting their woods."

"You help to protect the humans?"

"Yes, but it's not entirely philanthropic!" Seamus answered, his voice rising. "Have you ever eaten a big, husky black bear before it settles down for the winter?" Seamus put two of his claws up to his teeth while making a kissing sound. "So good!"

They both laughed at this last part. Seamus laughed because he hadn't spent this much enjoyable time with another dragon for as long as he could remember. And Maggie laughed knowing that the male had just opened up to her in ways that went against his primitive male thinking. He had let his guard down. He was vulnerable. And that was hot. Hot as dragonfire.

"Well, you'll have to share some of this black bear meat with me some time," Maggie said coyly.

"It's a date," he replied.

Several hours later, as the Sun's rays flickered through the branches of the nearby trees one last time before disappearing over the horizon, Maggie was curled up in a chair by the woodstove. She was halfway through a rather salacious scene in this raunchy book which Sparu had lent her and found herself oddly infatuated. She didn't normally read such trash, but it was captivating, and she refused to put it down until she hit the last page.

The story was about a workaholic divorcee who never did anything for herself until she one day snapped and mentally disconnected from the world around her. She traveled to a strange land for a fresh start, seeking all things which had been held from her for years. The protagonist indulged herself in every whim and desire, disregarding all repercussions of her actions. And when she least expected it, a quiet, distant man entered her life who understood her every need and whisked her away.

Wait a minute.

"Sparu, you're such a delightful, caring, ass," Maggie said aloud to the empty room.

Putting the book down, Maggie reached toward the side table next to her and wrapped her claws around the steaming keg of green tea. Breathing the wafting vapors rising from the semi-translucent surface of the liquid. She held the keg closely to her snout, reveling in the aroma of the delicious steam rising up and through her sinus cavities. She had added a clawful of raspberries to the cauldron while brewing and loved the extra flavor profile that it contributed to the mix.

Holding the tea in one claw, she grabbed her laptop with the other and pulled it over and onto her blanket-covered thighs. Setting the keg down after another intoxicating mouthful, she opened the screen and logged into her email. Clicking "Compose New Email", she quickly typed out a message to her neighbor back home.

> **From:** *maggiethedestroyer@dmail.com*
> **To:** *kotakthebenevolent@dmail.com*
> **Subject:** *So, I think that I'll stay a while…*
> **Body:** *Hey Kotak! Thanks again for keeping an eye on my place while I'm away. Contrary to what I told you before, I think that I'll actually stick around a little bit longer than I had originally planned. I'll have a moving crew come by to pack up my things and bring them up to Maine for me. Please let them in when they arrive. I owe you one!*
>
> *Thanks again for all of your help and putting up with me as a neighbor ;-) Hope that all is well! Maggie <3*

Closing the laptop, she carried the blanket and tea over to her bed and curled up in the middle. Hunkering down into the soft, deep bedding, she pulled her tail in close under the blanket and cocooned herself. She didn't know what lay before her, but she knew that she was finally on the right path. Closing her eyes, she quickly fell asleep, dreaming of a happier tomorrow.

Chapter IX

"So, what's the deal with Seamus?" Maggie asked nonchalantly, well, at least she tried to sound nonchalant.

"Seamus?" Sparu whispered back, ducking around the corner into the kitchen to stay out of ear shot of the other dragons eating breakfast. "What do you mean?"

"Well, you know."

"No, I don't know," the other female retorted, a grin creeping across her face. "I think that I *might* know, but I want to hear you say it."

Jumping into the kitchen and rounding the corner so that they were both out of view from the patrons of the inn, Maggie squealed with delight in finally getting to have some girl-talk time with her old pal. This hadn't happened in centuries, and she was ready to burst with excitement.

While she had fallen asleep rather quickly the night before, she awoke shortly after midnight and then laid there for hours staring at the weathered ceiling of her personal cave, dreaming of Seamus and their hypothetical life together. She had begun to plan their wedding, what they'd call their whelps, wondered if she could even still lay some eggs, that is, and how they'd spend their later years together. There was only one thing standing in her way.

He was 'maybe' married?

"I mean, is he available? Maggie continued, once she was sure that both her and Sparu were out of ear shot of anyone dropping eaves out in the dining room. "He wears a ring, but when we talked, he made it sound like he has been alone for many years. So, what's the deal?"

"Do you remember when you asked me before if he was single or not and I said that he wasn't?"

"Of course. The conversation is burned into my brain."

"Well, I technically told you the truth," Sparu explained, opening the lid to the dishwasher. She moved back to let the hot steam rise out of the opening and to the ceiling of the small room they were occupying. The warm rush of detergent-filled air hit Maggie in the face as it escaped the stainless-steel cube. "He's technically not single, but he's not really married."

"Explain," Maggie said, the curiosity oozing from her sly voice.

"He is married and still wears the ring," Sparu began her explanation, "But everyone knows that she's dead. I mean, he could start dating again if he really wanted to."

"What?!" Maggie screamed, covering her mouth with a free clawed hand. "What do you mean she's dead?"

"He didn't tell you?"

"Tell me what?"

"His wife was a fisherdragon for many years," Sparu continued. "She worked the sea while he tended to the lighthouse. They both followed in the respective clawsteps of their families and took up their trades from a very young age. Seamus spent his nights keeping the torch lit out on the humans' little fake island in the harbor, keeping the ships safe from the dark, elusive shoreline. She, in turn, spent her time sailing the deeper waters off the coast here catching fish to sell to the humans. Depending on the time of day, Seamus was very often out there protecting her and her crew while she was bringing home the bacon for them."

"Bringing home the bacon?" Maggie asked curiously.

"Oh, it's an old human expression," Sparu replied, laughing. "It means that she brought home the money. You know, the gold. I sometimes forget that you've spent most of your life around just dragons. I occasionally get some of the tiny creatures in and around these parts, so I've picked up some of their lingo."

"Okay, but go back a second," Maggie stated, her face revealing the strain of mentally calculating a slew of new variables being added to the equation she was actively trying to solve. "You said *was* a fisherdragon. What does she do now?"

Sparu just stared back at her, quietly contemplating how to answer. Sighing, she said, "Officially, she's still a fisherdragon. But she was lost at sea over two decades ago."

"Oh no!" Maggie cried out. "That's terrible."

"Tis," Sparu conceded. "She and Seamus were foundational members of the community here and her loss was felt throughout many circles. But it's been especially tough on Seamus most of all."

"How so?"

"Well, he's never admitted that she may be dead," Sparu replied after another long sigh. "If you ask him, which I do not recommend you do, he'll tell you that she's still out to sea and he's just waiting for her to come home. I'm not saying that he's delusional, but he's definitely aware of the truth and can't bear to bring that thought into his clouded reality. Left to his own devices, he'll continue on for the rest of his life thinking that she's still out there catching fish and destined to come home each night."

"That's awful," Maggie said, looking down at her clasped claws.

"Ugh, I mean, it's cute," Sparu said, leaning back and putting a claw to her forehead. "Shit, it's dreamy. I would kill to have a dragon love me that much. But, yeah, it's a little hard to watch sometimes. I've gone over to his place on the lighthouse before and found that he keeps the table set with a place for her ready to go. I've heard rumors that it's changed out daily to keep it clean."

Maggie continued to stare down at her claws, not knowing what to say.

"Tiamat, I'd let him shine his lighthouse over my rough seas any day," Sparu said.

Maggie turned to her and smirked. "You're gross!"

"Oh, please! Do you know how long it's been since a boat came to dock in my harbor? Do you think my ancient husband is looking to stick his oar into my dark waters every night? He can't even make it past the evening news. I'm sorry, but I have needs, too!"

The two dragons laughed, causing such a ruckus that some patrons out in the dining room got up to look around the corner at them. Quickly composing themselves, the two grabbed whatever random kitchen items were nearby and pretended to look busy. Maggie found herself to be stirring a tea pot with a slotted spaghetti spoon while Sparu was scrubbing an empty keg with some steel wool. Their faces frozen, they continued to stare blankly at the intruding curious patrons while continuing to perform their prevaricated tasks. They held their poses until they were alone again.

"Hah! Did you see the looks on their faces?" Sparu

blurted out. "This is why dragons keep coming back to stay here. There's always something entertaining going on."

A few days later, which felt like forever to Maggie as she continued to dream about their improbably future together, Seamus knocked on the stone portal to her guest cave. She had spent the morning buffing her scales and polishing her horns, hoping to impress him with her natural beauty. It had taken her over two hours alone just to get her scales to shine the right color, adding that special pop when the sunlight hit them at just the right angle. Her motivation throughout all of it was that he was going to put in just as much effort in an attempt to woo her.

She was quite mistaken.

He showed up looking, and smelling, like he had spent the morning working in the yard and picking up every variety of dirt and sweat local to this region of Maine. She wanted to be annoyed. She wanted to be pissed at him for not caring as much about their date as she did. But she couldn't.

It was kinda hot.

He stood in front of the door, a wing's span away, staring back at her. He felt so far away yet close enough that she could have reached out and wrapped her yearning claws around him if her inhibitions had been lowered just a hair. Looking him up and down, she noticed just how dusty and grimy his body was from a hard morning's work. The shallow angled rays of sunlight streaking through the surrounding trees reflected and glistened off his sweaty scales, bouncing up and into her eyes, showing her the color and tone of his rough yet handsome protective layer.

"Good morning, Miss Maggie."

Maggie stared back at him, unable to speak. She wanted to speak. Heck, she knew of a thousand different things which she could say to this ripped hunk of dragon standing before her. But in all the years of running programs, keeping meetings on track, and organizing professional teams on difficulty levels far exceeding that of herding cats, she finally found herself unable to articulate a sentence's worth of words.

"Maggie, are you alright?" He prompted, a look of concern growing across his definitively handsome facial features. Damn him and his rugged good looks.

Shaking her head, Maggie stepped back from the doorway. As if shielding herself partially behind the edge of the stonework could actually help to deflect the ridiculous position in which she found herself. Gripping the edge of the door jamb, she steadied herself from the anticipated crash she was predicting thanks to the lightheadedness washing through her scale-covered veins.

"I, um," she began, unsteadily. "I'm good, sorry. Just haven't had enough coffee yet, that's all."

She couldn't see it herself, but he had full access to the sheepish smile growing steadily across her face. She couldn't remember the last time in which she'd been so stupidly smitten with someone based out of pure physical infatuation. Maggie knew next to nothing about this male but wanted him so badly. She knew only rumors about his marriage and a sparse understanding of his job, and all of this was told through the gossiping shenanigans of Sparu.

Yet, she felt like a girl in college all over again when she was around him. If they had been at a bar, she'd have gone out of her way to encourage him to ask her to lead her shy little self back to his cavern to bang her against the wall until she passed out from the sheer pleasure of it all. She'd even wake him up the next morning with breakfast from a nearby coffee shop and leave later on without feeling embarrassed or remorseful for giving in to her carnal delights with a total stranger.

The confused look on his face when she finally focused her eyes again on the dragon before her told her that she'd stopped talking long enough during her daydream to weird him out once more. Or at least cause him to question her sanity. Or question his sanity regarding why he was at her door calling upon her for what may or may not be a date.

Which, she needed to remind herself, was probably not a date in the first place. Not that she was going to let that hold her back from having a good time…

"Well, this should help," Seamus said, handing a steaming wooden keg to her.

It took her another moment to recenter herself and remember what the hell they had been talking about. He smelled great. Well, disgusting, but tantalizingly attractive. She continued to stare at him and take in the sight of that sweaty sheen of light bouncing back to her yearning eyes from the morning Sun off of his glistening scales. Smelling the breeze blowing off his gorgeous backside, she caught a waft of coffee. Black.

Deciding to play it cool and put him on the spot, well within the web of her spidery game, she acted as if she didn't want the drink. You know, the drink that would rush enthusiastically-desired caffeine into her bloodstream and revive her skulking self back into a semblance of a living creature.

"Oh, is that hot coffee?" she said, coyly. "I've always been more of an iced coffee drinker. But thank you, though."

Smirking, Seamus didn't miss a beat. Bringing the well-worn edge of the keg to his lips, he downed the steaming beverage in one long pull. Setting the container down on the tree stump to his right, he brought his other hand around from behind, revealing two other kegs in his possession. From the way that he moved his claws, she could hear the jingle of ice cubes within the wooden confines.

"How about an iced coffee, then?" He asked, taking a sip from one of them.

"Well, only if it has—"

"—five milks and four sugars?" he interrupted. "I asked Sparu how you liked it." Nodding in satisfaction at the taste of his concoction, he took another long pull of the caffeinated goodness.

Blushing, she could just imagine the kinds of things that old hoot might have told the rustically smooth-talking male. It was clear from her recent girl chat with her friend that she was trying to simultaneously warn her about the dragon's sad past while also trying to get her to rattle his bones.

"And what, pray tell, did Sparu tell you in regard to how I liked it?"

Seamus spit his mouthful of coffee into the air before her. He thankfully had the wherewithal to quickly turn his head to the side beforehand, thus saving her clean scales and dignity in the process.

Smirking, she looked up at his coffee-dripping chin and dreamt of him kissing her with that toothy grin of his. She couldn't believe that a male such as he could have remained available for so long. He was stoic, brave, strong, yet humble and vulnerable in his feelings. He didn't try to hide things like her other mates had in the past. That is, of course, if you discount the tale of his marriage.

"I'm sorry," she said, smiling and coyly turning on one clawed foot. "Was it something that I said?"

Quickly composing himself, he flicked some dribbles of coffee from his chest scales and wiped the fluid from his chin with a swift swipe of his forearm. Maggie used to think that this kind of lazy, slob-like behavior was gross in a younger man but watching this muscled hunk of dragon before her do it so casually with the trained practice of a being who was used to living a rough and tumble lifestyle was downright erotic.

Tiamat, he was hot.

"I, uh, no, I felt a cough coming on right as I swallowed," he lied.

"Do you often gag when trying to swallow?" Maggie inquired. "I've never had that problem."

What was she doing? She never used to talk like this. But every time she found herself within eyesight of this male, she did everything in her draconic power to literally throw herself at him for the taking. She barely knew the dragon, yet she just alluded to her mastery of oral pleasures for absolutely no reason whatsoever.

If he had still had a mouthful of coffee, it surely would have been spit out once again. Thankfully for him, and her cleanliness, he had yet to take another sip. All that was evident from her innuendo was a smattering of beet-red blushing scales adorning the side of Seamus' face. In all her years of courting males for broodmates, she didn't think that she had ever thrown another dragon so hard off his game.

Looking down the ground, the sky, the trees surrounding the bungalow, and pretty much everywhere else that he could possibly look without having to make eye contact with her again, Seamus floundered as he searched for the right words.

"We, ah, we should get going," he finally mustered, his cheeks burning with the influx of blood pressure. "The early dragon gets the meat, after all."

"Well, I do like meat… and I can wake up early when I need to," Maggie said, sly. "But I'd rather stay up all night."

Averting her gaze, she couldn't bear to look into his eyes anymore knowing how awkward she had just made the encounter. She wasn't completely ashamed, though. After all, she was being rather truthful in your admiration, or infatuation, of the male, but she had to admit that she was coming on just a little too strongly so early in the game. If things were going to proceed in any semblance of success for her in her pursuit of his requited affection, she'd need to shift down a few gears before she completely drove him away.

"After you," she replied, motioning with a wing for him to lead her forward.

She loved having a male lead her when they walked. Don't get confused, she hated it when a male told her what to do when it wasn't his place to do so. But, if he was the target of her desire and she felt comfortable with him doing so, she sometimes liked to be a little submissive.

He dipped his head in acknowledgement and swept himself away from the door. His wings curled in to wrap around his sides and his tail swished over the ground, clearing the way for her to step out of the small, single-dragon bungalow and join him outside.

Looking up to the sky as she walked to join him, she marveled at just how beautiful of a day it had turned out to be. The treetops above created a living, continuously swaying green frame to the most wonderful shade of blue surrounding their little world. She had never imagined moving up here full time to live out the rest of her days but spending time in Maine on a day like this, she could live here for the rest of her life with no regrets.

And it would also help if she had some companionship.

"So, where are we off to today?"

Seamus paused before answering, clearly still thrown off his rocker by her absurd and extremely forward comments just a few moments ago. But he was still walking with her, and very close by, so she obviously hadn't screwed things up completely. Well, not yet, at least.

"Well, I can think of a number of good hunting grounds to take you to," he began. "But it really all depends on what you're craving."

Don't do it, Maggie. Don't open your Tiamat-damned mouth and push him further.

"I'm open to anything," she replied. And she meant it.

"Well, I mentioned bear the other day. Have you ever had a fresh bear straight from the forest? I know that you've been used to a more refined diet coming from the city."

"I've had bear before, true, but never fresh," Maggie replied. "I've heard that their warm blood is something which truly can't be described with words alone and needs to be experienced firsthand."

"I know of a few good hunting spots for bear, both brown and black."

"Oh!" Maggie exclaimed. "And moose. I've never taken down a moose and really want to try one. I've heard that they can get pretty big up here."

Seamus chuckled. "You better believe it. The moose around here, especially as you venture further away from populated areas, can get almost as big as a juvenile dragon. They're quite a sight, and good eating when you know how to toast 'em correctly."

Maggie bit her lip just enough to let a little trickle of blood ooze down her lower lip. All this talk of meat, fire, and tearing the life from her prey, all while coming from the mouth of this dreamy male was going to push her over the edge if she didn't do something about it. Better to cut to the chase and get a move on before she fainted from anticipated pleasure.

She just had to decide on which of her pleasures she was focused on. Hunting for game now with Seamus and getting her kill on, or trying to potentially develop a relationship with him, or jumping his scales and moving right to the finish line all battled for priority in her mind. The latter, while obviously enticing and her desired goal, had a lot of anticipated ways in which the plan could go wrong. If she pushed him too soon, she might lose him all together. It was better to play it cool.

"Let's go bag one of these black bears of yours," she

said, the blood still slowly trickling from her lip. If he saw it, he didn't say anything.

An hour of flying later, they approached a small green island and came down to alight in an open field near the center. Touching down in the soft grass and vegetation covering the fertile ground, she relished the feel of the tiny blades of grass and the random leaves and flowers against the bottom of her feet. Sure, there was that one thorny bush hidden in there, but her tough scales barely acknowledged its presence.

Plus, she squished it upon landing. Take that, thorns.

"So, where are we?" Maggie asked between breaths.

The flight wasn't that long, and she was in admittedly okay shape, but the air was starting to get cooler, and it burned on its way down to her delicate lungs. She had spent much of her life in warmer climates and was still adapting to the chillier temperatures found here on the Maine coastline. Granted, she loved it here, but it was taking a small toll on her body while she struggled to adapt.

"This, my lass, is Deer Isle, as the humans so dubbed it centuries ago," Seamus replied. The usage of lass sent shivers of excitement through her scales.

"What's a deer?"

"A deer is, well, used to be, a smaller cousin of the moose that we now consume as only delicacies on special holidays," he answered, somberly. "Deer were a thriving species in these parts up until the Great Rise. Our kind enjoyed eating them alongside the wee humans who also hunted them for sport and consumption, but as our numbers increased—"

"—So did our hunger for them," Maggie finished for him.

"Exactly."

"So, we drove them to extinction?" Maggie asked, a hint of sadness in her voice. She couldn't recall ever seeing a deer, let alone a photograph of one, but she'd eaten the meat in certain dishes over the years.

"Unfortunately, yes. That is why we now carefully control the hunting of certain protected species out here in the wild, like moose, bear, etc. Pretty much all of the apex predators… aside from us. With most of humanity out of the way, our will power to not just eat everything in sight will make or break the continued survival of many animals on this planet."

Maggie looked down at the ground, a forlorn sensation spreading through her body. She absentmindedly scratched at an odd-looking patch of dirt with one of her claws as she tried to ignore the ramifications of their discussion. She'd eaten meat her whole life and never thought twice about where it had come from and what affect her menu choices would have on the environment.

"So, we're going to go kill more of these rare animals today?"

"Well, yes and no," Seamus began. "We are going to go out and find a tasty lunch, compliments of the hunting knowledge and prowess of yours truly, but we're only going after bears on a specific island that's overpopulated right now. I have a license for two bears this season, so this is perfectly legal and sanctioned by those watching over the population of the creatures. And, regardless of legality, I know that this is the most ethical way to go find one of these furry morsels, so it helps me to sleep better at night… with a full belly, to boot."

It still unsettled Maggie a little. The bears were awfully

cute. But she did love the smell of freshly charred meat, followed only by the taste of said meat sliding down her throat while her teeth and claws were covered in the animal's rendered fat and blood.

So, long story short, she got over it pretty quickly.

After pondering his words for a moment, the smile previously adorning her face returned and she looked back up into his eager eyes. He had been watching her closely while she weighed her options and contemplated their act. She could tell that he obviously wanted her to come but would have cancelled the whole thing if she had been against it. There were few male dragons who would do that for her, and she knew it.

"Let's go, then," she said, smiling up at him.

A short while later, the two dragons circled the island just above the lowest layer of wispy clouds lazily drifting above. Seamus had told her that it was the perfect place from which to hunt. You were just high enough to see everything down below and with decent cloud coverage to mask your presence to all but the keenest eyes. She had never hunted bears before, but the concept was similar to other hunting methods which she had seen employed.

Maggie had grown up in a relatively food secure environment with parents who took care of everything. Being the youngest of her brood, she had been whelped through most of her early years and had admittedly not had to do much to ensure her survival until she had gone off to college. Even then, she had made a decent income with her work on the weekends to afford to purchase food with no need to go out and hunt it. Hence, she was essentially learning how to actually hunt for food for the first time, something all dragons should know how to do from birth.

She was glad that when this moment came, she had the pleasure of learning from this rugged male in the prime of Vacationland.

Gliding along on a warm updraft rising from the Sun-warmed ground below, the two dragons followed the currents in lazy circles above the green mass doting the dark blue ocean. Staying in close formation, they were often flying so closely together that their wingtips were practically touching. She even found herself at times drifting closer to him in the hopes that they would touch. When she did this, she noticed that he was actively drifting away, maintaining a close distance to her while staying just out of reach.

One time when she was feeling particularly daring, she gently arched her wings to pull the outstretched tips a few inches closer to her body. It didn't seem like much to the casual observer, but as she had found out over the years, a few inches could make a world of difference when used correctly. Drifting closer to him once again, she quickly allowed her wings to relax back to their full length and graze across his midflight.

The sensation was tantalizing. The smooth touch of his taut skin flaps sliding over hers sent shivers down the length of her wings and into the core of her body. The exhilarating feeling of knowing that he didn't try this himself but had allowed her to make this move coursed through her mind. Blood began pumping into places it had not been sent in more years than she cared to admit to herself. Turning her head from her observation of the ground below, she looked from one potential prey to another.

Looking to her right, their eyes locked for the briefest

of moments and she found him gazing back at her with as much curious intensity as she imagined she was conveying herself. His wing seemed to flutter in the breeze and gently caressed hers. Was it actually the wind making his wing move or his muscles under his control? She didn't know. But the feeling was all the same and just as glorious.

That is, until he drifted away a few feet once more, breaking the brief yet thrilling contact. He was just far enough to make the act seem like a natural occurrence riding the unpredictable air currents moving over the brisk oceanside island, but close enough to make his point clear: he wasn't ready.

But she was. Every scale on her body was ready for this, ready for something new, something fresh. Ready for him.

If he had wanted her when she first started flirting with him, she probably would have brushed it off as just some male horniness shining through like it always does with his gender. But the fact that he didn't want her, at least not obviously, was intoxicating. While she didn't see herself as some trophy broodmate one might show off at parties as a sign of male dominance over the surrounding lairs, she knew that she looked pretty damn good for her age and could woo a member of the rougher sex when she pleased.

But to not have her feelings equally requitted, and even worse, to be politely pushed back upon like he was doing to her now… was utterly enthralling. If he didn't reply in kind sooner than later, she was going to have to take things into her own claws… one way or the other.

Realizing that she had been awkwardly quiet for too long since the brushing of their wing tips, she decided to break the ice and dive into the next phase of this little trip.

They had spent quite some time now simply circling the island and staring down at the grounds below. She needed some hot, tasty action and wanted it now.

"So, not to sound impatient, but what's the longest that you've ever waited to go for the kill?"

Startled by her choice of words, which she regretted almost as soon as they passed by her finely-honed teeth.

"Excuse me?" he asked, looking at her questioningly with one eye.

"To kill a bear," she blurted out, trying to correct herself before the conversation spun off in a different, yet eager direction. "How long do you typically wait to kill a bear? It seems like we have been circling for quite some time now. Does it make sense at some point to just drop in on a known location where they typically live and just rout one out?"

Seamus cocked his head at her as he considered her words. Glancing to the Sun, he shrugged and turned back to meet her eyes.

"Well, the little buggers should be out by now to forage for food," he began. "However, they might have noticed us circling in the sky and are remaining under the cover of the nearby tree cover. Want to go down and poke around?"

Excited to be finally getting the show on the road and see some action, she grinned and shook her head in the affirmative. Nodding back, he leaned into a dive and rocketed toward a dense copse of trees down below. There was a small break in the leafy canopy, and he appeared to be aiming for it. Billowing her wings slightly to add in a little drag, she fell behind the massive profile of her hunting companion and sideslipped right. She rode so close in behind him that she could have stretched out her neck and nibbled on the tip of his tail.

She kind of wanted to, just to see what he would do. But she held back, no sense ruining the good cheer in which they both found each other at this moment.

Following in his wake, she found herself to be falling faster than before as she was cruising through the vacuum left in the wake of Seamus' bulk of muscles, scales, and teeth. She needed to induce some drag once more with her wings and tail in order to not completely ram him from behind.

Then again, maybe he'd like it.

"Stop it!" Maggie grumbled to herself, scolding her aroused thoughts.

"You okay back there?" Seamus yelled over the wind ripping past their bodies. "Am I going to fast?"

Not fast enough, she thought.

"No, I'm good! Go as fast as you like!" She yelled, waiting for him to turn his head back to the ground before allowing her mouth to curl into a grin.

They raced downward, barreling toward the break in the tree canopy, which from what she could tell, would be just big enough for their bodies to slip through if they tucked in their wings. Would they have enough time to slow down before hitting the ground? She'd normally be freaking out at this point, but she found that the more time she spent with Seamus, the more she could innately trust in him. Their prey was down there, and he'd see them safely to it.

Approaching the opening, he waggled his tail side to side to get her attention. He began to gently slow down, so she added some more drag to her profile and matched his speed, respectively.

"As soon as we pass through the canopy, break off in whatever direction is open between the branches and drop down beside me," he yelled, more clearly heard now that they had decreased their speed.

"Okay!"

"Watch my fingers," he said, holding his left hand out far enough for her to see.

He had three fingers extended. Tiamat, she could think of things to do with those three fingers. Focus! She scream-thought once more.

"When I get to zero, puff out your wings and prepare to land hard!"

She nodded back as he was watching her through their decent. He gave her a little wink and turned back to the rapidly approaching hole in the leaf cover. His fingers waggled and the three became two. Then one. Then none.

Dropping back as soon as she saw his last finger retract, she wanted to break her speed as quickly as possible in case he was able to slow down more rapidly than her. Maggie watched in awe as his gigantic wings shot out sideways just before they would have hit the trees and he instantly shot back toward her. She followed suit and marveled at how deftly he tucked them back in once more. He shot through the opening and disappeared into the black undergrowth below.

Half a heartbeat later, she did the same.

Before she knew what was happening, her world turned into a blur of greens, brown blurs, and black swirls inundating her senses. Her vision was slammed with hundreds of distractions, some immediate and in her path, while some were just far out enough to not be a concern.

Leaves, small branches, and thinly twisted vines scratched at her scales and raked her face as she plunged through the dense canopy. Even though they had entered the opening in the leaf cover, it was not the wide-open entry way for which she had been hoping.

Instinctively, she placed her arms before her face in the hopes of blocking any of the more painful pokey bits. Maggie's brain was overwhelmed trying to process everything entering her visual range and she yearned to simply close her eyes and hope for the best. But she knew that would be her downfall.

Sliding her nictitating membranes over her eyes, she regained her courage and managed to take in the world around her. She watched as thick branches loomed before her, threatening to smack her in the face if she didn't dodge ahead of time. Seeing Seamus break to the right toward a larger opening in the chaos, she juked to the left where she saw another opening appear which was just big enough for her more slender body. Tucking in her wings, she blasted through the gap in the branches, scraping up against the trunk of a large white oak tree as she blazed through.

Sensing an opening before her, she shot out her wings in a hopeful effort to drop her speed. She immediately felt herself slow down and the deadly feeling of a thousand tiny knife-like branches raking across the delicate membranes of her wings. Flaring her promethium glands, Maggie launched a salvo of flaming death down below.

Staring into the resultant conflagration, she revelled with glee as the dried spruce needles and wispy branches flared up before her and quickly turned to ash. Bracing herself once more with her scaled arms, she burst through the cloud of ash and debris, emerging on the other side unharmed and unencumbered. Her glee, however, was short lived. Emerging through the haze, she saw her next hurdle, and this one was impenetrable.

The ground.

Flinging her wings out as far as they would stretch, she flexed her membranes and put as much surface area as she could between her and the air below. Feeling herself slow, she pumped her wings as hard as she could, arresting the fall to the rocky dirt below as much as draconically possible. Seeing the ground still racing toward her, she belched the hottest stream of fire conceivably possible by a dragon of her kind, softening the rock below as she slammed into the ground before her.

Dropping onto one knee, she drove a clawed foot and two fists into the ground with a tremendous might, digging a small crater into the earth in the process. Rocks, dirt, decaying biomass, and anything else in her way flew up and outward, showering the nearby area in the detritus of her fiery entrance.

Heaving her lungs as rapidly as they would pump, she sucked in as much cool, fresh air as the atmosphere would allow. The smoke and airborne fire didn't bother her much as a lifetime of fire breathing had hardened her organs to the feeble allergens long ago, but she did have a hard time with the fine particulate of dusty rocks and dirt mingling in the air. Coughing the tiny invaders from her lungs, she peered through the dusty cloud in search of her partner. She started to panic as she realized that she couldn't see further than a few inches from her face.

Had she gone blind from the inferno? Had she looked into the flames too long? She didn't think that it could harm her, but mother had warned her long ago not to sustain a blast for too long and definitely do not look directly at the center of the stream where the temperatures were the highest. Or was it the dust? Was she blind? Permanently blind? Or just momentarily hindered as her body adjusted to the influx of environmental changes.

Breathing in and out more rapidly now, she felt that for the first time in as long as she could remember, she was having a panic attack. She breathed heavier and faster, with each breath coming more labored and forced than the one before. Vertigo assaulting her brain, she dropped further to the ground in the vain hopes of surviving this uncomfortable dizziness. Reaching out with a claw, she felt around for nearby trees, rocks, or even the ground below, just anything which she could rest herself upon until the world could stop spinning for long enough to regain her senses.

The dust swirled faster and faster, circling her face, and threatening to clog her nose and mouth, suffocating her for all of eternity. Wasn't this supposed to be a fun day out with a cute guy? Wasn't she supposed to be on a date, or non-date, if she could ever figure out what the heck they were doing today? Was it really going to end like this? Swiping her clawed hands before her, she tried to push the air out before her to rid herself of the dreaded particles, but the action only seemed to generate eddy currents in the air, trapping her more deeply within its terrible confines. She tried to flap her mighty wings and fly to safety, but she was losing her sense of orientation and didn't inherently know which way was up. She felt the ground below her clawed toes, but she didn't trust her senses enough to know if this were true.

Recoiling from the multipronged assault to her

nervous system, she thought that she had finally pushed herself too hard and would pay the price. She couldn't take anymore and knew that a few more moments of this and she would suffocate and die on this very spot. Flailing about for something, anything at all, to grab on to and orient her within the world around her, she finally saw her salvation: a dark blur emerged through the haze and thrust itself before her face.

It was a claw.

Reaching out for the strong clawed fingers of the well-callused hand before her, she gripped as tightly as she could with both hands onto Seamus' and let herself be yanked out of the cloud. Lifted from her feet, she accelerated outward from the fiery pit which she wrought upon herself and flew into the clean air beyond.

She thought that her body would be flung off and into some rocky terrain out of view, only to escape one deadly trap and fall unbeknownst into another, but her motion was quickly, yet gently, arrested. Maggie looked down the length of her arm and met Seamus' gaze at the other end. He flexed his muscular frame and swung her around, narrowly dodging a mammoth tree trunk and several nearby boulders. She rode the momentum, both frightened and enthralled by the sensation of riding on the end of Seamus' might limb. Biting her lip, she dreamed of what else she could ride on with him in control. Even on the verge of a blackout, her mind was stuck in the gutter.

Coming around, he brought her back to the dark, rich earth below and gently set her down on her feet. She relished the feeling of the cool, damp soil below, but already missed feeling him so close and so present in her life. Maggie couldn't recall the last time in which she had felt so out of control and fearing for her well-being but loved the feeling of knowing that she was safe in his arms.

Standing on two feet now, she stabilized herself and looked up from the now-steady earth and up into his deep eyes. She was a little relieved to see that he was out of breath, as well.

"Are you alright?" she inquired, panting as she struggled to catch her breath.

"Ha!" he laughed, or at least it mostly sounded like a laugh as he was too busy wheezing. "Am I alright? What about you? You almost lit yourself on fire!"

"What do you mean?" she asked, her defenses immediately going up as she looked back at him incredulously. She had seen and breathed in a great deal of smoke and ash, but she didn't think that fire was a major player in her freshly embarrassing moment back there.

"What do I mean? Maggie, you were nearly on fire! You created this amazing inferno as you fell back to the surface but ended up lighting a pile of dried branches and pitched-coated pine needles in the process. The whole ensemble caught fire and fully engulfed your body within the epicenter. I couldn't see you for a bit back there!"

Maggie simply stared back at him in a decidedly odd mixture of confusion and disbelief. Looking over to where she had landed, she stared in awe at the catastrophic damage she had wrought upon the land. A naturalist at heart and lover of all things living, it pained her to see how much of the forest floor she had obliterated in her ill-conceived fiery landing.

Finally catching her breath, she stood back to her full height. As hungry as she was, she couldn't let the fire burn on its own. She raced over to ground zero, ripping down burning branches and smothering everything on fire in her path. Stomping a particularly annoying cluster of embers, she walked back to Seamus feeling accomplished.

Gazing around at the forest floor, she saw that they were in the middle of a grove of oak and fir trees lining a steep cliffside leading to the hill above. Looking up the length of the wall, which was nearly vertical in some spots, she noticed a handful of fuzzy black spots moving along sporadic ledges in the rock. Continuing her scan, she detected several similar shapes moving along the base of the cliff off behind Seamus.

Looking up into his eyes, she whispered, "I think that they know we're here."

Turning slowly, he moved his head just far enough to let one eye take in the seen to his back. When his gaze returned to her, he had a devilish gleam in his eyes.

"You hungry?"

She nodded.

"On three," he whispered back. "Run toward the cliff wall. I'll break left, you go right. Grab whatever looks good, and we'll meet up for lunch."

He held out his right claw with three claws extended.

"This again?" she quipped. "Can't we just book it and go get roast some bear meat?"

Looking at her with an expression somewhere between confusion and dismay, he gently shook his head and shrugged in defeat. Raising his head, he sniffed the wind and squinted his eyes in contemplation.

"Last one to the bears is a laggin' dragon!" he blurted out as he spun and rushed toward the cliff wall in the distance.

Watching him disappear in a blur, Maggie dug her

claws into the rich earth and threw herself in his wake. She pumped her wings and ran with all the power which her legs could muster. Gaining enough speed, she was able to get sufficient air under her wings to create a modicum of lift, just enough to lighten her exerted mass on the ground and propel her body to its maximum ground speed. She'd love to fly at this point, but the trees were too close together, and the air was considerably dense due to the higher humidity in the cool shade of the thick forest. This combination didn't typically bode well for fliers such as she, so she kept her feet on the ground and eyes on the prize.

Seeing Seamus begin to veer off to the left as proposed, she leaned to the right and banked around a huge mound of rocks blocking her line of sight to the bear which she had been following. Swooping around the mountainous obstacle, she regained a visual on the creature and watched as it doubled back, heading toward where Seamus had just chased his prey.

Maggie tucked her wings tightly to her body and blasted off toward the quickly moving morsel on all fours. She tore through the forest undergrowth, flinging a trail of pine needles and black soil behind her as she raced in pursuit of the quickly moving bear. Ducking as branches reached out for her eyes, nose, and mouth, she shook off the attacks in her blind primal rage.

Sprinting across the dark undergrowth of the forest floor, she realized that she wasn't just hunting the bears for food. She was hunting them to prove herself to Seamus. From the moment she had met him, it was obvious that he valued a salt-of-the-earth gal and wasn't looking for some floosy from a high society dragon family. He wanted a female who could fend for herself and breath fire with the big boys. If she couldn't catch a bear on her first try and roast the living crap out of the thing, she would be telling him that she couldn't catch her own damn food nor provide for her man if she needed to. While she historically did not give too much concern to what the males of dragonkind thought of her, she did value this one's opinion just a little bit.

Okay, a lot of bit, she had to admit to herself. There was just something about Seamus which she couldn't shake.

But she also wanted to try some bear meat which she had hunted, killed, and roasted for herself. She had never actually done this before, and the concept intrigued her. Plus, she was not going to let Seamus know that she had never done it, nor that she had little to no clue how to even begin. She did, however, know how to run like hell and breathe a torrent of deadly fire. All things considered, that seemed like the main two characteristics a seasoned hunter needed for this little escapade.

Snapping out of her moment of conscious reverie, she put her game face on. The next few moments would decide many things for her, both personal and romantic. While she knew that he wasn't looking for someone per se, nor was he technically available, Maggie wanted him to think that she wasn't just some prissy pink dragon left to die as she waited for a strong male dragon to come rescue her from a lonely cave burrowed deep within a mountain. She had grown up reading fairy tales depicting damsels in distress hiding from the terrible human knights coming to kill them, with their only hope of survival being a courageous male flying in to scorch the knight to ash. While she had enjoyed the stories as a young whelp, she quickly realized that they were complete humanshit, and it was the polar opposite of everything which she aspired to become in adulthood.

Hence why she now found herself rummaging through the dense undergrowth of a remote island in the frigid state of Maine trying to find a stinking little ball of black fur simply to win a male's affection. What had happened to her? She never would have done this years ago!

Barreling through a copse of fir trees, she picked up the pungent aroma of her target and saw bear-sized paw prints veering off to the right. While she was no tracker or ranger of legend who could sniff a trail and taste the damp earth to detect what had passed by, when, and in what direction they had traveled, she did have common sense. Seeing the pine needles flung off to the left with deeper impressions in the dirt on the same side, she readily gathered that the creature had flung itself to the right and tried to throw her off by running around a pile of rocks adjacent to the well-worn trail they were on.

Taking the cue from the diminutive animal, which may prove to be her future meal if she stayed on course, she rounded the rock pile and zig zagged through a tight passage. The small thoroughfare, which she quickly realized was a well-travelled route through some fallen boulders raining down the cliffside over the years from erosion, snaked along the edge of the cliff and brought her around to the other side of the miniature mountain. The bear clearly knew where it was going and most likely presumed that it would be an easy way to rid itself of this fire breathing terror coming to ruin its day.

Jumping over several rocks which had left gaps large

enough for the bear but too small for a dragon, it dawned on Maggie that she was chasing prey trapped in a confined area—and that she could fly. Leaping up and onto a flat boulder to her right, she cleared the canyon and took advantage of the open space to stretch her wings. Flexing outward and giving them a few quick beats, she lifted off from the rocky terrain and took to the air where she was more in her element.

Soaring along the winding path, she kept herself a mere wingspan above the opening to maintain a lookout for the furry black bolt of lightning which had somehow managed to evade her up until this point. Pouring on some additional speed, she saw a blur up ahead and positioned herself for a better view. Seeing the target in range, she let off a burst of fire, aiming straight for the bear.

And it completely missed. It had been so long since she had hunted anything outside of a grocery store that she forgot how time and speed were related to each other. Her fireballs, while magnificently flamey and scorching everything that they touched, hit the spot where the bear had just been a moment before. Granted, the thing probably got a few singed hairs on its bottom to remember the near-miss by, but it was still a miss, nonetheless.

Thinking back to her mother teaching her how to hunt as an older whelp, she remembered that she needed to track the motion of the prey and anticipate where it would be when the flames reached the target location. It had been so long since she had belched fire with the intent to actually hit anything that she was a little perplexed on how to go about targeting the moving beast at this range and speed. So, she did the only thing that she could think of.

She belched a ton of fire.

Flying swiftly on the creature's tail, she let loose one gout of flame after another, each time moving her aim a little further in front of the animal's position where she thought the thing would be next. She missed every Tiamat-damned shot for the first dozen or so and would have gotten discouraged if it weren't for the fact that she missed a little less each time. Each shot went a hair to the left or right of the dodging varmint, but it nudged just a little closer with each successive attempt. Each shot threw the animal just a little further, cooked a few more hairs than the time before, and possibly scared a few more raisin-like poops out of the thing's soon-to-be roasted backside. Maggie almost had the thing, and she knew that suppertime was nigh.

Rounding a bend in the path, she found herself on a straight lane of open rock heading toward a sharp curve in the crevasse. If she could just catch up with the bear now and scorch the little bastard before it got to the end of the chasm, she could nail the bugger and prove herself to Seamus in one glorious shot. Pumping her wings harder and faster, she urged every ounce of her draconic form forward and into the optimum position to deliver the killing blow. Matching speed with the creature and then advancing upon it as she gained a few feet of elevation, she mentally calculated where her fireball would hit and positioned her skull inline for the shot. Warming her promethium glands, she readied herself to unleash her pent-up rage against this poor, defenseless little bundle of tasty meat. Narrowing her vision, she focused in on the target, took a deep breath…

And was slammed from the right into the cliffside

next to her. Maggie never saw what had hit her, at least not right away. She, did, however, note a distinctive red hue surrounding the blur of motion in her peripheral vision right before it careened into her like an out-of-control cargo dragon trying to haul a load of goods through a harsh storm. Her wing crumpled against her side and she was thrown into the rock face so hard that she momentarily lost track of where she was. Up was down, day was night, and left was right. She had no clue where she was or how long she had been laying there, except for one thing: she knew the face of the dragon below her.

Waking up a short while later, Maggie found herself to be laying on her stomach and staring at the cliffside to her right. Boulders were strewn about, blocking her in against the cliff on her left side and above her head, leaving only her tail end free to the open air. She could have asked someone what had happened, but there were only three witnesses to this train wreck, and two were dead and one had taken off, running for his life. Gently lifting her neck, she tried to raise it from the ground to crack the stress out of her vertebrae and rejuvenate her senses when she froze in her motion. There, immediately below her and currently supporting her body, was the groggy sack of muscle known as Scorcher, the Fire-Hearted, or more accurately, Seamus the Semi-Conscious.

"Uggghhhh," he managed, struggling to open his eyes. He faltered with trying to open two, clearly still dazed from the impact. So, he eventually settled on keeping one eye closed while carefully opening the other to look around.

Too groggy to move, Maggie continued to lie prone on top his body and stared down at his face. Into his eyes... his deep, thoughtful, experienced eyes. Looking down into the depths of his pupils surrounded by a multicolored firework display that was his iris was breathtaking. Never had she seen so much life, so much past, both good and bad, cheerful and sorrowful, contained within such tiny globes of the dragon body.

Feeling that she may have overstayed her welcome, she gently placed the palms of her clawed hands against his chest. Carefully pushing down onto the rest of his body, she marveled at how hard and rippled his torso was. Her claws gently slid across his chiseled abdomen, tracing each line and crevice of the tiny scales. She looked down to watch her hands following the contours of his body, biting her lip to hold back the onslaught of raw emotions struggling to overwhelm her nervous system. Every ounce of her soul, every drop of her blood, and every fiber of her being screamed at her to slide down and mount him here and now.

It was unbecoming of a female dragon to take such a role, but screw that. She was her own dragon and would do as she damn well pleased. If he wanted it, she would take him here and now and burst past this dam of feelings which had been resolutely straining against her flames of passion since the day she first laid eyes on him.

Sliding down the length of his body, she brought herself lower and lower, passing her face by his neck, his chest, and on to his abdomen. Maggie craved the taste of his body and yearned to just lean down and bite into his scales. Still moving slowly and without fully giving away her intentions, she eased herself off of him a smidge just to relieve him of some of her weight. She didn't know where and how badly he might have been hurt from their collision, but it was clear that he had suffered worse than she. And if he wasn't banged up enough already, he was about to be.

Looking down at his delectable form as she approached his waist, she was disappointed to see that his little dragon hadn't emerged from the protective confines of his cloaca yet. If he was aware of the situation enough, or at least subconsciously responding to her presence and touch, she had held out hope that he might at least be aroused by all of this. Although Maggie had to admit, that hadn't stopped her before. She knew how to turn on a dragon faster than a gas oven in her kitchen.

Straddling his tail as she continued to move down his body, she saw him finally raise his head and look in her direction. Still groggy from the hit, he looked confused at first, probably unaware of why he was lying on the ground and what she may be doing. The look upon his face when he finally focused in on her and he realized what was happening spoke volumes.

He did not want this, not any of it. Well, at least not yet, she hoped.

Shifting her hands and feet to the ground adjacent to his body, she quickly shifted her footing back to the ground and threw herself from her perch atop him. She had tried to not put any pressure on him, but the groan emanating from his mouth said otherwise. Maggie had dreamed of hearing him moan like that, but not from the response of having some internal injury hastened by a horny dragon attempting to seduce him.

"You win some, you lose some," Maggie muttered to herself.

Shuffling back toward his head, this time with her feet firmly planted in the dirt of the rocky chasm, she sprung to his side by his long neck and cradled his head in her arms.

"Seamus, are you okay?" She asked, trying her best to use as soothing of a voice as she could muster, and not sound like a dragon with a severe case of blue ovaries.

"What… what happened?"

"What happened?" Maggie replied, a hint of mirth shining brightly through her words. "Some crazy dragon slammed into me as I tried flying through this canyon here and knocked me out. He then laid on the ground and pretended to not remember hitting me as he recklessly flew through my hunting territory."

Seamus stared up at her, his eyes going wide as his slowing waking brain began to comprehend her sarcastic explanation of the events from the past few minutes. He opened his mouth to answer but stopped short and gave her a wry smile.

"Are you talking about me?" He asked with a smirk.

"Maybe."

"Wait!" He exclaimed. "Where did the bears go? I caught you lunch!"

Maggie, having completely forgotten about the damned bears in the tumultuous exchange, felt her stomach rumble as she pondered his question. Standing up straight, she craned her neck around and looked off in the distance.

"Ooh! They're right there," she exclaimed, pointing with a wobbling claw. The adrenaline coursing through her bloodstream must still be playing havoc on her cardiovascular system. "It looks like you must have flung their bodies off to the side when you slammed into me."

Seamus struggled to move his neck around to get a better look in the direction in which she pointed. He couldn't see the two bears, but he believed her. "Oof, I'm going to feel that in the morning," he grumbled, trying to raise his neck high enough to see.

The grunting sounds and dizzying look upon his face spoke volumes to the pain he must have been feeling but was afraid to tell her. She wished that he trusted her enough to let her in and how she could help, if at all. Her former broodmate was just as closed off to her and it drove her insane. Why were males so stubborn?

Reaching down, she extended a clawed hand to the Seamus. She expected him to shoo it away and refuse her help, but she was mistaken. Upon the offer, he looked into her eyes, and she saw it. That spark. A tiny twinkle of appreciation and understanding. He was okay with accepting her help and not afraid to show it. This one simple move was so simple, such a tiny thing, that nothing should have come from her seeing the display. But the move was so rare for the rougher gender of her species that it was so tantalizingly alluring. Maggie felt dumb for even thinking this way, but it had been a while since a male allowed himself to appear vulnerable in front of her.

He gripped her hand and squeezed. Not a light, dainty squeeze like someone would provide who wanted to pretend to want help getting up off of the ground but was afraid to break the precious little bones in the hand of the fragile female. No, Seamus gave her a real squeeze, the kind that would be necessary should a dragon actually want assistance in lifting his massive bulk from the forest floor.

Maggie looked down at his hand in hers. She marveled at the image of her claws wrapped around his, and his around hers. It was wonderful to feel the warmth of his hand flowing into hers through the firm yet gentle contact.

His digits squeezing into hers sent ripples of excitement through her scales at the bounty of implications from this subtle expression of friendly contact. If she were helping another female up after falling, she would have thought nothing of it. But his touch, his masculine, firm, rough callused touch was exhilarating, and she didn't want it to end. But she knew that the longer she spent looking down at him and not actually following through to assist him in rising from the damp patch of pine needles and twigs would only make the situation more awkward than it already was for her.

She could have been staring down at their conjoined hands for one second or one hour, she would never know. But the feeling was there and there was no denying that something had just transpired between them.

Spreading her clawed feet in the dirt to widen her stance and prepare her body for the extra weight, she grinned at him and nodded her head. Seeing the replied nod, she squeezed his hand just a little tighter and pulled upward, taking him with her as she lunged backwards, leveraging his body up and forward in one smooth motion.

Having steadied himself in a semi-seated position with his other arm under him, he seemed to relax his grip on her hand, but he didn't let go. She had instinctively begun to pull away, knowing that in most normal situations it would have been the correct time to back away and give the other dragon their wingspace, but she remained. Maggie didn't want to let go, and apparently, neither did he. She smiled down at him, enjoying every second of this encounter and knowing darn well that it would probably never happen again. She had come on too strongly and would scare him away after this date, destroying their chances of another shot at love.

But at least she had tried.

Her eyes out of focus as she continued her ponderance, she snapped out of it and looked back to his face, settling on his eyes. His glorious, deep, probing eyes… which were staring right back at her. A mix of contentment and confusion played out over the pupils of his eyes, and she could tell by the creases in his scales around his snout and skull ridges that he didn't know what to do next. Their claws were still touching, still intertwined long past the point of necessity.

They both felt that this was right. They both knew that this was wrong.

Simultaneously releasing their respective grips, the two dragons retracted their arms to their sides, looking off to the side at some imaginary thing to avoid sharing another moment of eye contact. Maggie, having been standing on her own already, easily pulled her arm back to herself and stepped away. Seamus, though, having been sluggishly holding himself up with an arm lightly dotted in black & blue marks, forgot to maintain that arm's posture and dropped himself onto his back.

Maggie watched in stunned silence as he rolled back onto his wings and slammed his head into the dirt once more. Thankfully for him, there were no rocks there, this time. She lunged forward, ready to pull him up if the need revealed itself. She stared down wordlessly, unsure of what to do.

"Seamus, are…"

"Ha ha ha ha!" Seamus bellowed in glee, intermixed with a few uncomfortable grunts.

Maggie, sensing that he was clearly fine, although a

little banged up and probably embarrassed at this point, couldn't resist joining in. The two dragons laughed and laughed, both releasing the pain from the hunt and subsequent crash with the bears, as well as their moment of connection.

"What a freakin' mess, huh?" Seamus asked, not necessarily to Maggie.

He groaned as he pushed himself up off the ground and to his feet for the first time since the collision. Bent over, Seamus looked up at Maggie and laughed again, shaking his head.

"Sorry about all of that, lass," Seamus began. "I seemed to have gotten my bell rung mighty fine during that little fiasco. Thank you for your help."

"My pleasure."

"So, what do you say we wrangle up those bears and get them cooking?" Seamus asked, clearly having regained his mental faculties and appetite.

Maggie kind of wanted to just get out of there, but she didn't want to scare him away. She had made a fool of himself and had practically considered riding him while passed out, so it was quite past her time to skedaddle. But yet, he still wanted her around. And from what she saw, he obviously had some kind of inclination regarding her motives back there. Yet that didn't scare him off. Not yet, at least.

Also, she was getting pretty hungry. No sense losing a male and lunch at the same time if she could pull this one back together.

"I'd like that," she replied, genuinely happy for a change.

An hour later, the two dragons sat side by side in front

of a roaring fire. Stradling their make-shift fire ring quickly fabricated by the ever-resourceful Seamus, were two uprights with branches shooting off in a Y-shape toward the late afternoon sky. Nestled in the crook of each Y was a large diameter log tied to the deskinned body of one of the two bears. A lively fire started by their combined breaths and fed by an assortment of downed branches collected by the duo, was merrily cooking the bears and adding a rich, smokey flavor to the meat.

Maggie had never lit a campfire before and was fascinated by Seamus' instructions and tutelage. Of course, she had obviously started many fires in her day, but she had never gone through the trouble to procure appropriately sourced fuel and maintain the fire for means of heating or cooking. She had mostly lit other things on fire which she wanted to see obliterated and then reveled in its subsequent destruction.

Seamus had done a magnificent job with this little picnic, Maggie had to confess. She wasn't used to being with a male who knew his way around meal preparation, so the simple act of starting a fire and roasting an animal over it was quite the turn-on for her. While she had had meals cooked for her in the past by her former broodmate and other potential suitors, they had always felt forced and carried too much weight. This meal, though, was something different.

The two sat for a long time simply staring in the fire and nibbling on hunks of meat as they finished on the spit. Maggie had never sat and really appreciated the beauty of a fire before. In all her years, she had viewed fire as merely a tool to accomplish a goal. Now, she was able to see the raw power in the ephemeral substance, the font of heat and joy which emanated for all who would gather around and reflect upon its presence.

She had also never really had someone with whom to enjoy a relaxing night by the fire. Seamus, for all his talk of hard work and focusing on productivity, could really kick back hard and relax when he wanted to.

Leaning back, she put her arms out behind her and leaned against the ground until her wingtips touched the cool forest soil. She stared up at the sky and marveled at the varieties of blueish-white clouds wispily swirling high above their horned heads. There were light blues mixed with orange and yellow where the last vestiges of the sun's warmth still reached out to caress the cool early nighttime air. Watching longer still, she could just make out the sight of miniscule black and brown dots in the distant trees, the trace coloring of small birds and bats darting from one hiding spot to another.

Continuing her stare, obvious to all that was around her beside this spot, their slowly disappearing food as their nibbling continued, and Seamus, she completely lost track of time. It wasn't until the sky turned to a navy-blue background merging into her beloved daylight, robing her of the warm soothing sunshine when she even remotely became aware of what time it was. Or where her hands were.

Looking down, she noticed that as the hours had progressed and their day together dwindled to a sad end, their two clawed hands had slowly but surely moved laterally toward the others. Light scuff marks to the side of her palm showed just how hard she was leaning on that arm while still subconsciously trying to make her way over to the male adjacent to her. In the course of this flirty little journey, she had, apparently, placed one claw lazily over one of his.

And he hadn't moved away.

Feeling her heart beat more rapidly in her chest, she could feel her blood hotly rush through her body, flushing her veins and engorging all the right spots. Her amygdala lit up like a Christmas tree while her pituitary gland roared to life. Endorphins, oxytocin, and vasopressin flooded throughout her body, simultaneously relaxing her while tensing her body in ways it had never been tensed up before.

What was it about this dragon which set her heart, and other body parts, afire? He was technically unavailable to satisfy her whims, yet she continued to fantasize about what he and his talons would do to her if given the chance. He was still legally married, and as far as she could tell, completely disinterested in picking up anything that she was putting down. Maggie had never considered herself to be the type of female who could be a cave-wrecker, yet here she was ready to fight this missing mystery wife of his in the arena if it meant that she could have five minutes to thrash this dragon's body.

Lost in her daydreaming of the kind of night she could have with him, she hadn't noticed his hand slide out from under hers. Seamus had come to his senses, obviously noticing his lack of diligence, and returned to his normally proper gentlemanly behavior. She didn't know how long they had been not holding claws, but when she looked down and noticed the change, her heart sank ever so slightly.

Turning to look at him, she could see the shame in Seamus' eyes. He had been caught up in the moment just as much as she had, but he had far more to lose. He had a broodmate whom he loved, and to some small degree, had just cheated on her.

"Why couldn't she just be dead?" she thought to herself. "Things would be so much easier if he could just move on."

She instantly regretted the thought and felt ashamed of herself for even contemplating the notion. Her history with her own broodmate had been drastically different. When they had eventually parted ways, Maggie wanted nothing to do with the dragon ever again, safe for the occasional interaction involving their hatchlings. But Seamus… he was robbed of his love. Whether she died or left him, he had done nothing wrong and deserved better.

Looking back to him, she could tell that he had reached the end of his mental and emotional capabilities for this trip and would need to pull the ejection handle any moment now. She hadn't meant to make things awkward but had only wanted to give in to her cravings, her desires, and her affection for this dragon in the hopes that maybe he had felt the same. She was falling in love with him and couldn't hold back her feelings, even if she knew that it was wrong.

"Seamus, I'm–"

"I think that I need to get going," Seamus began. "Thanks for coming hunting with me today, Miss Maggie. Sorry to leave so abruptly, but I need to see to something back at the lighthouse. Must make sure that the fire is still lit and all. You know the way back to town, right?"

Getting blown off and being told to fly home on her own would have offended her coming from any other dragon. But not Seamus. She had wronged him, and she knew it. It was not necessarily her fault either, but this wasn't the time or place. She needed to let him go.

"Oh, of course," she said, trying to sound more cheerful than she felt. "No problem."

"Well, until we meet again," he said, dipping gently at the waist as he bid her farewell.

"Till then," Maggie replied, watching him fly off into the last sliver of the sunset. She stared in his direction until he disappeared into a tiny spec of black and then was consumed by the enveloping rays of the Sun. She hoped to see him again but doubted if it would ever come true.

CHAPTER X

A few days later, Maggie was sitting outside of her bungalow when Sparu passed by carrying a large bundle of firewood. They hadn't spoken since the morning of her hunting non-date with Seamus.

"Hey there, stranger! I haven't seen you in a while. Everything alright?"

"Yeah, I guess," Maggie muttered, taking a long sip of her flagon of green tea.

It had grown cold during her last few minutes of zoning out and staring into the green-black void of the edge of the forest. Looking down to see how much was left, she held it out by the tips of her claws and belched a small gout of flame into the inside of the vessel. A few drops tried to splash out from the invading conflagration, but quickly sizzled and evaporated before they could find a place to land.

Sparu cocked an eyebrow and looked down her snout at the other dragon. Maggie looked away, trying to ignore her, but couldn't maintain the act and finally met her gaze.

"Okay, it's not alright," she admitted. "I mean, I'm alright, I'm just cranky and in a bit of a funk."

"I'm guessing that your date didn't go so well with Captain McDreamy of the SS Lighthouse?"

"Har har har," Maggie replied, spitting her long forked tongue in the direction of her friend. "It wasn't a date; you were right. We had a great time, but then I kept making little advances and he would retreat in kind. The game went back and forth for a little while, but ultimately went nowhere."

Sparu looked down at her quizzically.

"It's only a game, you know, if both dragons are playing," she said. "Were you both playing a teasing little game back and forth, or were you hitting on him like a lonely high schooler at the mall and he was being a gentleman, a married gentleman, mind you, and politely refusing your advances?

Maggie stared back at her and sighed.

"That's what I thought," Sparu said. "Well, Miss Maggie, I think that there's only one thing to do."

"What's that?"

Sparu smiled. "You need to get laid."

Later that week, Maggie and Sparu meandered down the cobblestone path which served as the main thoroughfare for the oldest part of the town. While the stones were uneven and had most certainly seen better days, they were in surprisingly good shape considering that some portions of the walking path were over two hundred years old. And built by humans, if you can believe that.

The street had been the first attempt at paving a road for the tiny fishing village once it had begun to thrive, but soon proved to be dangerous for the tiny creatures' fragile bodies when pedestrians, humans on bicycles, and humans driving horse-drawn carriages all tried to share the same roadway. As can be expected, several of the wee creatures were squished under the wheels of a cart or the hoof of a horse. The deaths and stained cobblestones quickly led to the town leaders to decide that a half-mile stretch of the street should be blocked off to establish an area solely for the use of foot traffic. While some rambunctious lads and lasses tried to sneak through the gates at each end with their two-wheeled bicycles, the local constables quickly suppressed the notion by whacking the punks over the head or throwing them into their tiny little jails.

While the move had obviously been annoying for the out-of-towners in the beginning who were unfamiliar with the lay of the land, both tourists and residents alike agreed that it was the best course of action for human safety. Soon after, restaurants, small shops, and cute little boutiques began to pop up in empty store fronts all along the stretch of the walking path. This in turn led to a thriving economy within the village which miraculously pulled in out-of-town money for the normally self-sufficient fishing village. The new-found cash flow was spent to build bigger, better buildings along the path and streets further from the center, and the small village quickly grew into a bustling town.

That is, of course, until the dragons broke free of their secluded bondage and took their rightful place as masters of this land. Now the entire village was vehicle-free as all of the dragons flew from place-to-place if the distance was long or quickly strode on-claw from one point to another if it was close by. While there were some small bands of humans on the outskirts of the town, they mainly came in by bicycle when they were feeling brave and very rarely went near to a passing dragon.

And thus, that is how Sparu and Maggie found themselves casually strolling along the quiet pathway that Friday evening. They were in the lull between most dragons getting out of work to go home and heading out to hit up the hotspots of the town. Sparu referred to this time as 'The Calm Before the Storm' from her years of running the B&B with her husband, Ender. Normally she would be with him serving drinks and dishes back at the Drag Inn, but he had begrudgingly agreed to work the restaurant by himself. They were able to secure the help of some of the human cooks and waiters running amok between the legs and tails of the larger dragons on staff, so that Sparu could take the night off and help her friend.

"So, what exactly are we doing out here?" Maggie asked incredulously. She had yet to venture out into the village after sundown and preferred to stay home with a good book and a steaming barrel of tea. She had flown over this part of town when going from one place to another on errands or travelling but had yet to go downtown.

"Well, my dear, this illustrious part of our little hamlet in the North is where all of the oldest shoppes, restaurants, and peddlers of wares have set up residence," Sparu replied. "Some of these places are just a few years old while others have been around for hundreds of years!"

"That's not very long. What's the big deal?"

"Not very long for us," Sparu conceded. "But long for the weak little humans who originally built the structures. Most of them have been converted with higher ceilings and larger floor layouts to accommodate our body size, but some are still owned and frequented by the sparse human population. We try to live in harmony here, although a few of the little morsels do get eaten each season."

Sparu looked at her with a devilish grin and winked.

"And we're going to one of these tonight?" Maggie asked. "A human or dragon establishment?"

"A little of both, actually," Sparu replied. "We're heading to the oldest pub on the island, actually, in all of the state of Maine, affectionately called Old Flames. It was originally a human pub established just after a skirmish of sorts that they refer to as The Revolutionary War and has been in continuous operation ever since."

"Have the humans been running it this whole time?" Maggie asked. "I still get nervous anytime a human makes me food or drink. Well, maybe not much lately, but when I was younger and heard the rumors from my older relatives, I was always under the impression as a whelp that they would try to poison us."

Sparu laughed. "Perhaps that was a concern in the beginning after the transfer of power following the Great Rise, but not in many, many years. Now both humans and dragons run the pub, each working together to cater to their respective clientele. It's a rather well-oiled arrangement and the tourists seem to love it."

They walked along quietly for a few paces while Maggie contemplated her story and put two and two together.

"So, are you setting me up on a date tonight?"

Sparu smiled and shot her a raised eyebrow. "Not tonight, but I can, if you want."

"Ugh, I don't know," Maggie started. "I'm just not really in the mood right now."

"I understand, you're in a funk," Sparu began. "So, that's why tonight we're just going to go relax, get some drinks, eat some unhealthy food that we don't really need, and just get the lay of the land. Old Flames is where the real locals go, especially on off-nights when there are fewer tourists around. But tonight is a weekend evening during peak leaf-peepin' season, so you should have a nice display of both townies and strangers alike to scope out and ogle."

"Ha ha, thanks," Maggie retorted, feigning offense. "I'm not here to be creepy and stare at the males like they're pieces of meat."

"Fine, more for me to check out," Sparu returned with a wink.

Passing through the massive iron-banded wooden door at the front of the building, the two females walked down a short passageway leading toward the main section of the pub. They passed by a coat check, bathrooms, and several storage closets before coming to a hostess station. A younger, bored-looking dragon, barely beyond her whelp years, stood there chewing on a bone. Seeing the two females approach the station, she threw the bone over her shoulder and straightened up.

"Good evening, ladies," she said, welcoming them in. "How may I help you this evening? Would you like a table in the main area, a private room, or the bar?"

"Wherever the hottest single males are located," Sparu answered, elbowing Maggie.

The hostess laughed. "You ladies are hunting tonight, I see. The bar it is."

She grabbed two menus and swished about, her tail whipping around and smacking the wall on the opposite side of the passage. It was clear that the renovations since the Great Rise were mainly focused on improving the headroom for the dragons at the expense of width. While the current owners had been able to buy up several of the nearby properties to expand outward, they weren't able to make it as big as it would have been if designed for the larger bodied dragons from the start. From what Maggie could see, the first and second floors had been combined to double the ceiling height, with an expanded second story having been added where the traditional third story would be in a human-based home. It was cozy, if a little cramped.

The hostess led them to the end of the passageway and over to an empty spot at the bar. Two stools stood available, beckoning to the tired rear ends of the two females. The hostess dropped the menus on the bar top in front of them and scooted out of the way.

"Have a seat, ladies. The barkeep should be over shortly to take care of you."

"Thank you!" they both replied, taking their seats.

Maggie instantly fell in love with the place. It was rough and could use a thousand different small upgrades to make it feel like a normal restaurant, but it was perfect in all the right ways. From the rough-hewn shiplap boards on the walls, the exposed beams supporting the structure of the building, the quirky way that the floorboards warped from years of settling and expansion in the radical weather of the northeast, all the way down to the well-worn edge of the bar top, this place was special. The pub had all of the key features which were only obtainable through centuries of hard use by people and dragons who affectionately called the place home.

Taking one of the two proffered stools, Maggie ran her claws along the top of the bar and marveled at how well-oiled the surface was and the way it glowed in the dim candlelight from the rustic chandeliers above their heads. Despite the thousands of scratches and dents marring the surface, the wood was alive and warm, speaking volumes to the countless stories told in its presence.

"Do you want me to get you two a room?"

"Huh?" Maggie asked, snapping out of it.

Sparu laughed. "You and that bar top. Do you want me to leave? Do you need some privacy with that thing?"

Maggie's face flushed as the blood rushed to her cheeks in embarrassment. She hadn't realized how long or how in-depth she had been admiring the room and its furniture.

"This place is amazing, Sparu! Just look at all this wood. It's so alive. So warm. I've never felt so relaxed in such a noisy, crowded environment."

"You grew up surrounded by stone, didn't you?" Sparu inquired.

Maggie nodded affirmatively, still rubbing the bar top with a thumb and gazing up at the ceiling.

"Humans of the past loved stone because it lasted," Sparu continued. "But in the recent centuries, especially after the advent of their fire departments, humans adopted wood construction over chiseled stone. Most dragons grow up in caves, like yourself, and know only the cold, dark, damp environments found deep within the mountains and underground rivers."

"But wood… is so, so…"

"Beautiful," Sparu answered, sensing that Maggie

couldn't find the right word. "And that is one of the many appeals of this place and why we dragons took it over and redesigned it for our larger bodies. Most dragons would never dare construct an entire building out of wood for fear of an enemy, or a clumsy friend, burning it down. But not these humans. No, they built beautiful homes out of trees and those lucky enough to live in one grow to love them above all other options."

The two dragons continued their adoration of the room around their two stools. Sparu not as much, considering she lived in town and visiting regularly, but Maggie couldn't get enough.

"Good evening, ladies," a voice spoke from a wingspan away, pulling Maggie away from her daydreaming. "How may I help you this fine evening?"

Sparu, at least, had been paying attention and saw the gentledragon approach their table.

"Ah, Claudio! I haven't seen you in ages," Sparu exclaimed, excited to see her old friend. "How are you? Where have you been?"

"Miss Sparu, I didn't recognize you from afar," Claudio responded, gently bowing.

Claudio, one of the oldest dragons in the area, was one of the first to settle in this part of Maine after the Great Rise. He had quickly adapted to the life of a publican and took over the pub from the humans after they temporarily fled the region.

"I am doing quite well, my dear, quite well," he answered. "As for my little disappearance there, I had taken an expedition trip of sorts with our friend Kade to look for a new fishing spot for his fleet. Things were going well; we found a few nice spots where the fish would congregate, and everything seemed hunky-dory. Well wouldn't ya know, we got caught in a might squall and our boat started to take on water."

"Oh no!" Sparu cried, adding in some extra dramatic effect. As her friend was right before her, she obviously knew that the tale had an acceptable, if not happy, ending.

"So, what did you do?" Maggie exclaimed, suddenly interested in the tale from the stranger.

"Well, we bilged the water as quickly as we could, but just couldn't keep up," the male continued, his pace and voice rising as his enthusiasm for yarn-spinning increased with their expressed interest. "Kade even scorched some tar with his breath to try to warm it and spread over a crack which had formed from slamming into a great wave, but he ended up setting the boat on fire."

"Ah!" the two females said in unison.

"Ah, indeed. We fought to put out the flames by tossing more water onto the burning wood, but that only made us sink more. Eventually, our half-sunken mess of a vessel drifted clear across the gulf and dumped us out over by Meteghan."

"Meteghan?" Sparu asked. "Isn't that all the way over in—"

"Nova Scotia!" Claudio exclaimed, beating her to the punch. "Well, after all that, and the fact that the boat was bloody well torched, we abandoned it with the harbor master over there and just flew home. Hence, my disappearance and tired wings this evening."

"That's amazing," Maggie said. She knew very little about long distance sailing and was enthralled with the male's retelling of the events. "You're lucky to be alive!"

"Well, don't count me out yet, young lady," he

answered, a chuckle creeping through his words. "I may be old, but I still have a little fire left burning in my promethium glands."

Reaching under the bar, he produced two empty flagons and set them before the females. Filling them each with iced water from a barrel behind him, he gave them something to start with and quench their thirsts.

"Now, what would you really like to have tonight? I'm quite sure that you didn't come down here just for my company and ice water. We have beer, wine from the human-farm down the road, roasted moose, and pretty much anything else which you may desire."

Sparu jumped in first. "My friend here, now that you bring it up, definitely has desires. Can you bring her the hottest, sweatiest, most ripped piece of dragon meat that you have here in the pub? Something tall, dark, and handsome, maybe?"

Maggie spit out the mouthful of water she had just sipped between her deadly teeth. She shot Sparu a look which would have burned more deadly than the greatest gout of fire imaginable. Sparu had not, in fact, lied, but she didn't need to tell this complete stranger about it.

And, if she had thought that the older man would have been embarrassed by the exchange, she was dead wrong. Claudio, to her astonishment, simply laughed. It wasn't even an 'I can't believe she just said that' laugh, but more of a 'Good ole Sparu' type laugh, as if he had heard this type of shenanigans in the past.

"Sparu," he began, leaning back against the counter behind him, "I see that you haven't lost your touch. Let me guess, she's one of your friends from back in the day, has been single for all of a few weeks, and you're trying to get someone to rattle her scales before she heads back home?"

Sparu simply smiled, pointed at Claudio with one claw and pointed to the tip of her snout with another. She winked at Maggie.

"Well, miss—?"

"Maggie," Maggie contributed, before Sparu could butt in with more of her silliness. "You may call me Maggie."

"Or Magendron the Destroyer!" Sparu blurted out. "Tiamat, she was a real tyrant back in the day." She elbowed her friend, trying to get a rise out of her.

Claudio smirked, clearly glad to see his old friend up to her normal behavior.

"Miss Maggie," he said, obviously respecting her wishes at self-identifying through her short name. "I can't help you out directly, not at this time, at least. Anyone who I would have recommended to you were all snatched up and broodmated within the past year or so. But! I do have a possible option for you. There will be a speed-dating party coming up next weekend for singles here on the island. Perhaps you could meet a fella then."

"What's a speed-dating party?" Maggie asked, confused. "It's been a few centuries since I've been on the lookout for a new mate, so I might be behind the times a little."

"Ah, no worries there. It is something new that the kids have concocted," Claudio explained. "You sign up when you arrive and get paired up with all potential suitors matching your preferences in a round robin style. You spend a few minutes with each potential match, get to know each other through some back and forth with questions, have a few beers, hang out and relax, and see where things go. You fill out a little questionnaire as the night goes on and turn it in afterward. If you and any of the gents both indicate that you like one another, we let you know and you can discuss a future date with them directly if you so choose. If you don't like someone, then you didn't waste too much time and can go about your business."

"Hmm, that doesn't sound so bad," Maggie said after a moment of consideration. "How many male dragons typically show up?"

Claudio winked. "Enough to make it worth your while."

The following Saturday afternoon, Maggie knocked on Sparu's door and waited. She had spent all morning fussing over this and that and had finally reached the point where she would either go or give up. There wasn't much else she could do with what she was given.

The door flew open in a rush and Sparu charged through. "Ah! Look at you. You look hot!"

As much as could be seen through her green scales, Maggie blushed. She had spent most of her life working in a male-dominated world where females were always at each other's throats, often times literally, to work hard, be noticed, and rise to the top. When they should have been banding together to defeat the patriarchy, most of her gender conformed to the environment which they found themselves in and instead chose to fight amongst their own kind. Thus, Maggie wasn't used to compliments like this from another female. So, when it did happen, she was often caught off guard.

But, as she'd learned through their long friendship, Sparu was a kind soul who was quite different than other females. Heck, she was different from most dragons in general, and that's why Maggie loved her.

"Heh, thanks Sparu, you're too kind," Maggie managed. "But seriously, though, I look okay?"

"Dude, you look great," Sparu answered, looking her up and down. "You cleaned all that grit from under your scales. Your wings aren't all wrinkly. And you even cleaned the carbon scoring from around your nostrils."

"Hey!" Maggie barked, whacking her friend with her tail. "You know that my fire breathing is heavily carbonized and burns dirty. I've had doctors look at it and they can't do anything about it. Give me a break."

"I'm just messing with you, honey," Sparu said, laughing. She wacked her friend back with her own tail. "You're looking good, kid. Now, head down to the pub, kick in the door like you own the place, and go meet yourself some single males."

CHAPTER XI

"Good evening, ladies and gentledragons of Bar Harbor!" a voice struggled to break through the tumultuous din echoing about the inner room of the Old Flames. The gathered dragons were creating quite a ruckus and the speaker was straining her voice just to be heard over the crowd. She called out again, with little difference being made by her increased volume. In retrospect, she should have tried to do this sooner in the evening considering the event's two-drink minimum.

Looking to the poor female trying her best, Claudio shook his head and glanced around the room. A scant few of the dragons were paying attention, despite having paid to attend the festivities tonight, and even those rare sets of eyes barely looked to the speaker for very long. Climbing up on top of the bar, something which he typically frowned upon, at least in regard to the patrons, he went to work. A gout of glowing yellow and orange flames shot out from between his sharpened teeth, casting the room in a warm glow. The concentrated inferno leapt into the chaotic air buzzing around the room and flew over the heads of the patrons.

The crowd immediately fell silent, with a gaggle of dragons below and around the aforementioned jet of flame ducking or diving to the floor. From what he could see, several of the taller beings within the group had the tips of their horns singed ever so slightly. He hadn't meant to let the fire droop that low, but it happened to all dragons when they got older. He winced and gave the few a 'sorry' shrug before jumping back to the floor. The female looked over in his direction and gave him an appreciative, albeit a little fearful, wave.

"Thank you, Claudio, for your continued support and hosting our event tonight," she began. "Ladies and gents, tonight we will be running a round robin spree of speed dates for your mutually selected dating preferences. Thanks to the high turnout of you fun-loving dragons, each dragon present will get a good handful of mini dates throughout the evening. If you came to mix and mingle, then you are in the right place."

A few raucous woos shot out from various points in the crowd, indicative of the excited and horny nature of some of the participants. It could get lonely up here in the woods of Maine during the offseason, so this was one of the only ways to meet another dragon for many of the singles in attendance.

"Please line up and meet me at this table," she said, motioning to an old, heavy-looking wooden table dragged out of a dark corner by Claudio just before the start of the event, "and I'll distribute your dating cards. You'll meet with each potential date in the order indicated for five minutes each. And if we're all lucky, you might just find another dragon to meet up with afterward."

The crowd, clearly happy by the general buzz in the room and the onrush of excited conversations breaking out in unison, quickly queued up in front of her table to find their potential matches. There was no rhyme or reason to the order as the organizer had had little to no time to prepare for the evening. She struggled to sort through the names on the list and matched the cards to the patron before her.

A few of the patrons, seeing the long line, meandered over to Claudio for another drink before diving into the dating round. A little extra armor to brace themselves for the anxiety-fueled social event would do some well and probably mess up the nights of others. Claudio was always mindful of how much each dragon was served and did his best to limit those who lacked self-control.

Maggie, stepping up to the table as the dragon before her moved out of the way, smiled as best as she could to give the impression that she was excited to be here. Sparu had done a pretty good job of convincing her that this was a good idea, but she still had her doubts. She hated blind dates and this arrangement was just a dragon scale's thickness better than the former.

Reaching out for the card bearing her name when offered, she moved to the side and found an empty chair along the wall. Opening the folded card in her claws, she saw that she was paired up with ten other male dragons. While she was perfectly comfortable and often times sassy with other ladies, especially if wine was involved, she felt no degree of attraction toward her own gender and had faired heterosexually for her entire life. Well, there was that one night in college… but that didn't count.

Sighing, she resigned herself to accept this endeavor and try her best to have fun. She was simultaneously annoyed at only having ten other dragons to meet considering the size of the crowd here in the pub while also anxious at having to speak to so many strangers in such a short period of time. It was quite the paradox in which she found herself, all thanks to her inability to control her base desires. Damn hormones.

Looking down the list of males on her card, she thankfully didn't recognize any of the names. She had been nervous that she'd have to go on a mini date with someone whom she had met on one her few trips into town for food and supplies, especially if things eventually turned sour. This way, at least, if he wound up being a crazy drake and she wanted to pull the parachute cord on her voyage, she could bail out and minimize future awkwardness in her comings and goings. You know, more than usual, anyway.

"Ladies and gents," the organizer yelled out over the chatter. "Round One is about to begin. Please go to your assigned table and meet your first match. Have fun and good luck!"

Looking at the first line on her card, Maggie worked her way through the crowded pub and found her first table number.

Table 13.

"Great," Maggie thought to herself. Maybe if she were lucky, she'd go on a second date with this potential serial killer on a Friday night and wind up going the way of the human Templars. She shook her head and tried to snap out of it. Ever the master at self-sabotage, Maggie was apparently already looking for a way to make this go badly and then have an excuse for not having any fun. She decided that whether she had a good time tonight was entirely in her claws. If she were to ever get out of this funky rut and back to her good ole self, then she needed to cut the dragonshit and put her best claw forward.

Grabbing a pen from the table, she started scanning the list and prepared to take notes as she spoke with the queued up gentledragons. Obviously, the only way she knew how to treat this whole affair was like a business meeting. She'd find out what both parties wanted, what they were willing to trade to accomplish said goals and find a way to compromise to have everyone walk away at least equally displeased.

"What an ass," she thought. Maggie was really going to equate dating, sex, and even love with another dragon to a simple business transaction between two organizations. Had she really gone this long without feeling genuine love from another being that she couldn't leave work-at-work? Had she reached the point where she associated all things in her life as simple exchanges for goods and services with piles of gold coins and jewels?

Sensing a new color breaking through in her peripheral vision, she looked up to see a tall, pretty good-looking dragon appear before her. He sauntered up to the edge of the table, just next to the chair on the opposite side. Maggie attempted to greet him but didn't know what to say. Clearly sensing her social stumble, the male stepped in to save the situation.

"Hi!" he greeted. "Are you—" he scanned the list on his card, obviously not knowing her name as much as she didn't have a clue who he was. "—Maggie, uh, Magendron the Destroyer?" He was trying to hide it, but there was a slight chuckle seeping through his razor-sharp teeth.

"Yes, I am," she said, standing and offering him her hand to shake. He seemed to be confused by the offer, most likely expecting nothing at all or a friendly hug at most, and simply stared down at her hand. Sensing the confusion, she retracted her hand and greeted him by name, having read it from the list while he had searched for hers.

Sitting down, he scanned his card while looking up at her. "So, the Destroyer. The destroyer of what if you don't mind me asking?"

She did mind and answered him with only a glare through squinted eyes.

"Hi there, I'm Maggie. What's your name, what are your goals in this endeavor, and what do you consider a minimum goal in order to achieve success in the transaction?"

She spent the next four minutes and thirty seconds grilling him on his past, current situation, and future goals without giving him little more than a chance to answer each question with a sentence or two. Maggie hadn't meant to hog the entire conversation, but she had been classically trained in how to approach and commandeer a conversation for the betterment of her position. She had mentally prepared herself for this very situation and needed to remind herself that this wasn't a zero-sum game and both parties could theoretically win.

So, as one may be able to imagine based solely upon her opening salvo of job prerequisite questions, the first date didn't go very well. Nor the second. Nor the third. But on the fourth, she had learned how the game was played and started to loosen up a bit. Apparently, you didn't need to be on the defensive from Minute One, nor the offensive, and could actually trust several of these individuals from the inferior gender to speak up and tell her the truth. This was not something with which she had a lot of familiarity, and it would take her a while to get used to this.

And so, she proceeded through the rest of the

evening trying out her newfound relaxed approach. She would wander over to the assigned table, meet her date, and carefully grill him on the questions from her personally crafted dating-eligibility questionnaire. Maggie tried her best not to make it sound like an interrogation as she had with the first several males, but the underlying goal was still the same. The night dragged on as she slowly made her way down the list. A few of the males were attractive and very easy to look at, but even fewer were interesting enough to catch and hold her attention for most of the five minute get-to-know-ya period.

Bidding the second-to-last dragon on her list a good evening, she leaned back in her chair and resigned herself to leaving. This night had been a complete waste of time and she questioned the merit of sticking around any longer. Yes, she wanted to find someone nice to spend time with and possibly develop a relationship, but it just didn't seem to be in the cards for this evening. Heck, she would have been content to even meet someone who was brave enough to ask her out on a real date and simply make out for a spell.

But no. It was not meant to be.

That is, until he walked through the crowd. The last male on her dating card, a tall, sturdily built red worked his way through the throng surrounding the open floor adjacent to her table and emerged before her. Looking down to the number placard in the center of her table, his eyes slowly moved up along the length of her neck and settled on her eyes. She didn't realize it, but she hadn't taken a breath since catching sight of him.

"Good evening, Mademoiselle," the man spoke. "My name is Andre. Are you the illustrious Maggie who I have been waiting for throughout this entirely dreadful night?"

Maggie was never one to find herself without something to say. Whether it was a red-hot comment fired back at a co-worker, a snarky reply to a dumb question, or just a gossipy comment to a friend, she was always ready to socialize and keep the conversation flowing. But instead, this time, she simply stared back at him like a shy schoolgirl who was talking to a cute boy for the first time in her life.

"My apologies, my dear," Andre continued. Maggie realized that she didn't care what he was saying, as long as he kept talking. He could read the phonebook to her, and she'd be enamored with his smooth and melodic voice flowing into her ears. "I didn't mean to catch you off guard. May I join you?"

Wordlessly, she motioned to the empty chair across from hers and very obviously looked him up and down. Maggie was at the point of the evening where the bowl which she kept her shits to give was absolutely empty. She didn't realize it, at least not at first, but his scale colorations, shape, and physical muscle build was a slightly younger version to that of Seamus'. The feelings which she had for Seamus, and the things that she'd like to do to him, and have him to do her, erupted in her mind and threatened to take over all of her mental and bodily control.

After taking his seat, Andre's butter-rich voice poured across the table and carried Maggie's emotions, among other things, exactly to where she needed them to go. The two dragons made idle chit chat and covered the basic ice breaker details, but as the five-minute time alarm rang out, they didn't move a muscle. Their eyes never left the others as their newly developed bond grew deeper.

The other dragons around the bar naturally rose from

their tables and the volume of noise in the room rose with them. Greetings were called out from friends across the way, newly found friends, and perhaps more, said their goodbyes with semi-serious promises to connect again, while others silently slipped out of the backdoor before their dates could notice.

Claudio bellowed out offers of drinks and pub food to entice the crowd to stay. He succeeded in netting a few hungry stragglers, but most of the gathered crowd proceeded out the main door and into the cool night beyond. Taking a rag from below the wooden bar top, the elder dragon began wiping up some spilled drinks from the wood before it had a chance to ruin the smooth surface. He was just about to finish polishing a sticky spot on the edge when a female approached from the shadows and sat down before him. She held a flagon in her hand and placed it on the bar top, smiling at the male.

Claudio sternly stared back at her and without looking at it, reached off to the side and slid an empty coaster over toward the flagon.

She held his gaze with her own ice-cold stare, her expression unflinching, but quickly gave in and rolled her eyes. Lifting the vessel from the wooden surface, she waited for Claudio to slide the coaster underneath her claws before placing it back down.

"I just polished that area, my lass," Claudio, said, eyeing Sparu.

"You can polish my ass, if you like," the feisty woman said. "But, alas, you have my apologies. I wouldn't want to mar the surface of such a beautiful piece of wood."

"Does your husband know that you flirt so much and with such spicy language? And you know that I'm married, too, right?"

Sparu blushed and gave him a little side eye.

"Besides, I wouldn't even have the energy to keep up with such a young firecracker such as yourself."

"Ooh, you do know how to sweet talk the ladies, Claudio," she said, reaching across the bar to lightly touch his arm. "Where were you a few hundred years ago when I was a single gal?"

"Alright, alright," Claudio said, holding up his hands defensively. "There's a room upstairs, if you want it."

"Are you joining me?"

"No! It's for you to take a cold shower," he said, sticking his tongue out between his knife-like teeth. "Now, what can I actually help you with this evening? Would you like a refill on that drink? What did you have, a gin & tonic?"

Hand still on the flagon, she tilted it from side to side to see what, if anything, was still left. She sadly noted that only a few tiny pieces of ice had remained, but they were floating in a sea of melt water, traces of lime, and possibly some gin. Not wanting to waste her second-drink, she hoisted it to her teeth and dumped the remainder down her gullet.

"Ah!" she said, smacking her lips. "That was a good G&T. What kind of gin was in there?"

"You noticed, did you, my lass!" Claudio said, excitedly. "That's a new batch that just arrived directly from London, England. You can practically smell the fog on the barrel. It's supposed to be the best!"

Rolling the sweet fluid around in her mouth, she concluded that she could not disagree with his assessment. She wasn't sure if it was her favorite, but she'd consider trying it again.

"It is good," she said. "But I think that I've had enough for this evening. I mainly came here to snoop on my pupil over there and to see how she fared tonight." She motioned with the end of her snout toward the two dragons in the corner. "I've seen enough of her awkward courting and will be on my way home momentarily.

"Well, I'll be," Claudio whispered. "Is that the young lady who came in with you the other day?

Sparu slowly nodded in assent.

"Is she," he began, looking on in wonder, "is she trying to eat the face of that gentledragon there?"

Sparu laughed, banging the empty flagon on her knee. "That, my old and very innocent friend who obviously hasn't been out on an exciting date in a while, is calling making out. You know? Sucking Face. Snout Bumping. Necking. Tongue Twisting. Teeth Grinding. Kissing?"

"Yes, I'm not a total prude, you bampot," he muttered. Sparu placed her hand upon her chest in mock offense. "I have whelps and grandwhelps, so I've obviously mated a few times, at the very least."

"Good luck with all that mating tonight then," she said, motioning to the two dragons fondling each other in the dark corner. "Hand them a mop and tell 'em to clean up when they're done."

Claudio groaned. They better not try anything like that here in his pub. It was his job to get them socially lubricated, not support their actual mating rituals. Shaking his head, he looked to Sparu.

"Bye, bye, beautiful."

Already on her way out, Sparu turned back while still walking away. "Don't bother to write," she shouted back, waving as she disappeared through the front door.

Hastily jiggling her key ring, Maggie struggled to find the one belonging to her bungalow in the darkness. She couldn't see very well thanks to the New Moon and the lack of streetlights in this part of the park. Well, that, and the fact that Andre was behind her with his arms wrapped around her yearning self. His hands quickly explored her body with the skill of a dragon who had done this countless times before and the abandonment of a horny drunk male solely focused on things to come.

She wanted to protest. She wanted to push him back and tell him to be patient and to respect her modesty while out in public.

But screw that. It had been a while since someone had buffed her scales and she wanted this badly. Throwing all caution to the wind, she let him have his fun. Her muscles quivered in anticipation with each subsequent strokes of his clawed hands and she craved what was to come as soon as the door burst forth before them.

Finally finding the right key to open her lock, she thrust the long member toward the mouth of the cylinder plug. Feeling the tip hit off-center, she gently moved it around until the tip found its home. Carefully sliding it in, despite the vigorous jostling of Andre behind her, she pressed forward and drove the brass key into the body of the lock.

Starting slowly at first, she picked up speed and

pushed harder and faster as the key drove home. She could sense each pin rush upwards against the resistance of its respective spring, rising and clicking into place against the shear line of the plug. Breathing deeply, she felt the last pin click home with a thrill of ecstasy as the lock finally submitted. With the key buried deeply, each groove resting just right against the pins, she gripped it tightly and twisted. The door, lock, handle, and dragons, all burst forward, spilling the latter into the entry way of the home.

The two dragons flew to the floor, their wings and tails wrapped around each other's bodies in a drunken embrace of lust and passion. There was no love to be found here, only two horny dragons looking to take their pent-up aggression out on one another. They slammed into the floor and skidded to a halt just inside the swing radius of the front door, barely having time to get the last vestiges of their tails and wings through the portal before Maggie stretched outward and kicked the door shut.

One eye slowly opening to the squeal of wood and steel sliding on top of one another, Maggie's brain groggily ran through its wake-up routine. She had done this countless times over the years, except this morning featured one fairly prominent addition:

Wake up

Check to see if a sexy random French dude is in bed with you.

Use the restroom

Drink Coffee

Repeat #4 until eyes fully open

As one might imagine, the closing door and vacant warm spot in the bed next to her indicated that item number two on this morning's To Do List was a big ole negative. She lazily ran her claws through the neighboring spot and soaked in his latent body heat. His scent permeated the sheets, filling her eager nostrils with the aromas of his wings, claws, muscles, and every other body part she had sampled only a few hours earlier. Maggie wanted nothing more than to just lay there all day, filling her lungs with the smell of her lover, but she couldn't bear to see him go.

Jumping from the bed, she flung the covers out of the way and padded toward the door. She had seen countless romance movies where one lover snuck away from his or her one-night-stand before they awoke, looked over their shoulder, and stared back into the eyes of their yearning partner. Maggie wanted that feeling so badly and craved the emotional rush which she'd experience if only Andre would fulfill her one last fantasy on the way out. Even if she were to never see him again, just knowing that he was still thinking about her would spike her blood pressure in ways that she couldn't dream.

Approaching the door, she carefully gripped the doorknob and opened it inward, stepping out onto the front stoop. Off in the distance, she could just make out the silhouette of the male cresting the nearby tree line, soaring into the bright shining rays of the morning sun.

One hand rose to her chest, absentmindedly searching for the spot where Andre had gripped on tightly last night during one of their throws of passion. His claws had dug into the cracks between her scales and penetrated her soft flesh beneath. It had stung, but the pain had hurt in ways which she'd never experience before and would have been an idiot to tell him to stop. Just grazing the spot with her own hand now sent shivers down her spine as blood rushed downward into her awaiting loins.

Biting her lip, she watched in agonizing dismay as the shape of Andre's body got smaller and smaller, slowly disappearing all together into the far-off distance toward the East. Letting out the breath which she hadn't realized she'd been holding all along; she slumped back into the side of the door jam and let her head thump back into the wood. Closing her eyes, she took a deep breath and slowly let it back out.

"Ahem," a voice coughed out, mere feet to her right by the sound of it.

Maggie's eyes shot open, and she quickly turned her head toward the source of the sound. It was Seamus. She tried to speak, tried to form the words, any words really, but nothing came out.

"Good morning, Miss Maggie," the dragon said. His voice quavered with the effort of the four words. It was clear that he had not only been standing there the entire time unbeknownst to her, but that he had probably watched Andre leave the bungalow only moments before her appearance. "I'm sorry if I'm, uh, intruding on you and your—guest."

Maggie continued to stare at the dragon, only summoning enough strength and fortitude to look more widely and take in the scene. Seamus was standing there holding a large to-go flagon of steaming coffee and a satchel. From the smell wafting off the bag, she surmised that they were fresh baked blueberry muffins from the small bakery in town.

"Seamus," she begins, stumbling over the simple words. "I, um, I can explain."

"No need, miss," he stammered. "I heard that you had gone to one of those crazy dating events last night and thought that I'd swing by to bring us, I mean, you, breakfast to help cheer you up. You know, those things can be a waste of time and leave you feeling more alone than before you arrived."

Maggie tried to talk, but nothing would come out.

"I'm just going to leave these here for you," he said, holding the bag and flagon out for her to take. When she didn't immediately move to receive them, he awkwardly stepped forward and gingerly placed the items on the stoop in front of her.

"I'm going to leave now," he said as he turned. "Good day, Maggie."

Seamus stalked off toward the clearing, pumped his wings more quickly than usual, and took off into the cool morning air. He didn't look back, didn't say anything else as he flew into the sky.

Maggie rushed forward, tripping over the coffee as she ran, spilling the contents onto the ground below. She ran into the clearing in front of her bungalow and yelled out to the dragon disappearing beyond the trees. "Seamus! Seamus, I'm sorry!"

She watched as he left, the second time that she had done so this very morning. One male had left after having his way with her, most likely never to call again. The other left out of personal embarrassment for falling for the wrong girl.

Turning around, she looked down at the mess of food lying before her. The coffee was mostly empty and had created a large, caffeinated puddle at her feet. Sighing, she picked up the flagon to drain what remained and the thankfully still-clean satchel of muffins. If she was going to be sad, she might as well get fat and happy in the process.

Shuffling up the walkway, she gripped the door and slowly closed it behind her.

CHAPTER XII

Giving the worn wooden surface of the front door to Maggie's bungalow another rap of her knuckles, Sparu sighed and leaned back from the entrance. She had knocked several times now and given the female an ample period to come to the door, but it was no use. There was smoke coming from her chimney, so she had to be in there. Sparu placed her ear against the door and listened. It was hard to tell, but she swore that she could hear music coming from within. Stepping back, she sighed again, staring at the locked-up home of her dearest friend.

Her dearest friend who hadn't left the house in nearly two weeks.

Sparu wasn't sure what had happened but given that Maggie had not left the bungalow since the night of the speed dating event down at the pub, and the fact that Seamus was skulking around like someone stole his cookie, she knew that something was amiss. That's why she decided to finally barge in and see what the hell was wrong with Maggie. Besides, she still owned this tiny house, and she didn't want her friend stinking it up with her dingy body odor. It would do the gal some good to get out in the fresh air and soak up the sunshine.

Carefully setting the tray down on the bench beside the door, Sparu gasped as the flagon of orange juice almost tipped over. The benches around this place were a few seasons past their prime and had started to sink deeper into the soft soil. They were neither solid nor load-bearing at this point and would need to be replaced before the next round of tourists arrived.

Turning back to the door, Sparu fished the keyring from her pocket and found the one belonging to Maggie's house. Unlocking the door, she retrieved the tray and quietly pushed the portal open with her tail as she stepped up and over the threshold. Kicking the door closed, she took in the scene before her as the music and stench assaulted her senses.

Dirty clothes were strewn about and looked like Maggie's dresser had blown up. Shirts were hanging randomly on chairs and the table, shoes were kicked all over, and every other article of clothing imaginable was covering the floor as far as her eyes could see. A stack of oil-soaked pizza boxes sat haphazardly near the door, accompanied by an adjacent semi-smashed pile of wine bottles.

"What have you been up to, girl?" Maggie asked out loud.

Turning around, she couldn't bear to look upon her spoiled building any longer and vowed to slap some sense into the girl. Setting the food down on the coffee table in the center of the living room, she walked over to the staircase and made her way up to the second level. It was from up there that the music seemed to be coming, more specifically, the bathroom.

Placing her claws upon the banister, she looked upstairs and called out. "Maggie. Maggie!" Hearing no response, she decided to head up and investigate. Slowly padding her way up each step, careful to only touch down on the ball of each foot without letting her clawed toes click on the wood, she progressed upward until she found herself at the top of the landing.

Stepping over another pile of dirty laundry, she crept up to the closed bathroom door. The music was definitely coming from within and only further hampered any sound of Sparu's travels. She couldn't tell what was going on inside and she was certain that whoever was in there didn't know that she was outside the door. Cocking her head, she tried to focus on the music. Her English comprehension was remarkably high given her role within the tourist industry, but her knowledge of human music was a scale's thickness on the slim side.

"Wait a minute," the female said to herself, pausing longer to listen. She found her clawed foot to be tapping on the hardwood flooring as the beat sunk into the core of her brain and dug up old memories. "*Work it* by Missy Eliot? You are an unusual creature, Magendron the Destroyer."

Raising her hand to the door, she gave it a gentle knock.

Nothing.

Shrugging, she grasped the doorknob and slowly turned it, pressing against old wooden door as she moved forward.

The door was stuck. Looking up at the top of the door jamb, she could see that the wood had swelled from the hot steam on the other side.

"Tiamat damn you, girl," Sparu swore under her breath. "I told you not to take such hot baths with the door closed."

Pressing her shoulder against the door, she pushed

hard against it. The door didn't budge. Backing up a foot, she braced her feet against the smooth oak floorboards and threw her bulk against the bathroom door. She slammed into it just above the doorknob, bashing the door inward and flinging her into the room beyond in its wake.

Mutually frozen in sheer terror and surprise at the sudden appearance of the other, both females just stared at each other. Maggie had obviously not heard the other female coming up the stairs, and Sparu, in her wildest dreams, had not anticipated seeing what she saw in the tub. Well, maybe that's going a little extreme—she'd often dream some pretty wild stuff— but she was surprised, nonetheless.

Unsure of what to do or what to say, Sparu tried to be the mature dragon here and turned away. While she wasn't a stranger to what she had just seen, it was the first time that she'd seen another female in the middle of the act.

Laying there, in the tub that she owned and would need to deep clean prior to the next guest arriving, was the sprawled-out form of her best friend. Maggie was lying on her back, with her right leg up in the air against the wall of the bathroom and her left draped over the edge of the clawed-foot tub. Wings curled around her torso and her long neck perched against the other wall, the female seemed to be completely at peace with herself, at least until Sparu had barged in and ruined the moment. With one hand deftly probing her cloaca, the female was working the shower wand back and forth, alternating the massage and pulse settings on the wand as she did so.

Despite the shocked feeling rushing through her veins, Sparu couldn't help but note how well Maggie seemed to be adjusting the controls with one hand while using it to… shower herself.

And thus, the hysterical laughing began. Followed by a death shriek from her friend and an MP3 player being hurled at Sparu's head. Quickly spinning toward the door, Sparu's tail swished around in an arc, nearly smacking Maggie in the face, but not before catching the shower curtain. The material caught on to Sparu's scales and ripped away with a raucous tear. Her tail pulled the hanging rack and plaster from the wall in the process, cascading a plume of dust and chunks onto Maggie below.

Still laughing, Sparu ran from the bathroom and started down the stairs. Having stepped on the slick, damp tiles in the bathroom, she made it only a few steps before her feet slipped out from underneath her. Ducking her head between her arms, she defensively curled into a ball and rolled down the last flight of stairs, crashing into the pile of pizza boxes near the door. Her tail slapped around as her acrobatic routine concluded, slamming down into the haphazard menagerie of human-made wine bottles. A rainbow of glass shards flew through the air, bouncing harmlessly from the protective layer of Sparu's battle-hardened scales, before tinkling to the floor in a chaotic kaleidoscope of absurdity.

Aware that several spots on her body were in pain, but still laughing manically at the bewildering sight of her self-exploratory tenant upstairs, Sparu wriggled on the floor for another minute until she heard the creaking of the stairs above her. Coming to a stop, she laid her head back on the floor and looked up to the most embarrassed expression ever to be seen on a dragon's face. Maggie stood there before Sparu, her body now wrapped in a towel, with her eyes gazing anywhere and everywhere but Sparu's face.

"I'm, uh, sorry."

An hour later, the two dragons were sitting at an outside table in front of the Tooth & Tail, a local pub down by the water. It was an upscale gastropub by night but served a delightfully quaint brunch in the mornings. Sparu liked to come here from time to time when business was good but couldn't afford it much more than that.

Taking a sip from her flagon of mimosa, she pretended to look down at her menu for the hundredth time since they had sat down. The offerings for that morning were written in chalk on a precision-cut-but-made-to-look-rough piece of slate like all the upscale places did these days. Humans and dragons alike loved to pretend they were in an old fashioned, down-to-earth setting while paying a week's earnings for a fancy-looking breakfast.

Holding the piece of slate in her claws, she glanced down at the specials artistically drawn in organic, free-range something-or-other chalk that the establishment's owner boasted about hand selecting from some free trade chalk mine on a tiny island off the coast of France. She had even heard the dragon once refer to it as 'the essence of calcium sulfate'.

What she really knew, though, was that it was regular old chalk bought from the hobby store in the next town over sloppily written on pieces of slate from the hardware store by the owner's husband. The things that people do to trick tourists…

Peeking over the upper edge of her faux blackboard, she surreptitiously looked over at Maggie, watching the female and trying to gauge her mood. She was obviously embarrassed, a little pissed off, and probably annoyed that she didn't get to finish herself off before Sparu intruded.

If Sparu was being serious with herself, it was probably the latter that bothered Maggie the most. Well, that and having your best friend walk in while you were pleasuring your egg hole with a shower wand.

She decided that it would be up to her to break the silence first. Although, she figured that she'd have a little fun first.

"So, you come often?

Silence.

Sparu cleared her throat, pretending that nothing weird had been said. "Do you come here often?"

Maggie slowly took her eyes from her menu and looked into Sparu's for the first time since back at the bungalow. The other dragon slowly raised one clawed hand, extended the middle finger, and then retracted it.

Sparu smirked. "I am so glad that we did this," she continued, her confidence building as the snark-train left the station. "I've had such a good week so far, but this really is the climax."

Silence.

Looking down at her menu once more, eyes never leaving the over-priced chalk characters emblazoned upon the dark gray surface, Sparu launched another passive-aggressive salvo toward her friend.

"Did I tell you that I found a fresh scratch in the side of my truck the other day? Thankfully, it doesn't look too deep, and I can probably just rub it out."

"You're such an ass," Maggie retorted after a long moment, finally giving in to Sparu's taunting.

The heckler laughed, content at finally poking the other hard enough to respond.

"Okay! I know, I know. I'm sorry," Sparu answered. "But that was funny."

Maggie glared back at her with a slight head tilt.

"And Missy Eliot? You were masturbating to a human pop song? Ha! I never thought that I'd see the day."

"Are you finished?"

"Are you?!" Another round of laughter from the older dragon. She couldn't help herself this morning.

"Seriously! It's not funny," Maggie roared back. Several of the nearby patrons looked her way and the dining area got really quite. Maggie lowered her voice and leaned in closer toward the center of the table. "Please! I'm serious. Can we drop this? I'm embarrassed enough as it is without you tossing more wood on the fire."

"Oh, I'm sure you'd love to have a big piece of wood tossed onto your fire."

"I'm not talking to you."

"Okay, I'm sorry," Sparu said, after catching her breath again. "No, really, I'm done. I am done. I swear. I'm sorry. This is clearly an awkward situation for you, for both of us, and I'm only making it worse by capitalizing on the moment while you're down."

"Thank you," Maggie muttered, staring daggers at her from across the table.

Sparu paused a moment before proceeding, not really sure what to say which didn't involve an innuendo poking fun at her friend. She had gotten her digs in and should be happy with what she got. Admittedly, it must have been embarrassing for Maggie, and she shouldn't push it any further.

"Are you okay?" she asked, settling on a friendly tact. "I haven't seen you out and about in a while."

"Yeah, of course. I mean, I guess?" Maggie started. "I'm okay, just a lot on my mind."

"Want to talk about it?"

"I don't know," Maggie began. "I'm just kind of in a funk—again. Ya know?"

Sparu assumed why but didn't want to interrupt. She nodded while taking another sip of the mimosa. She could tell that Maggie wanted to vent and just needed the proper venue.

"I had spent so long in a loveless bond, then found myself on my own with no cares left in the world, and suddenly, I started caring again! I told myself that I wouldn't fall in love, that I wouldn't give my heart to another bumbling idiot of a dragon who only wanted me for my body, and I was fully prepared for it. I don't need a male to make me happy."

"You're telling me," Sparu quipped, quickly averting her eyes as Maggie stared back at her.

"Yes, we know," she answered dryly. "Again, I'm sorry. I'll clean the tub before I leave. Tiamat, I'll buy you a new tub, okay?"

"Okay, I'm sorry!" Sparu said, holding her claws up defensively. "I'm done making jokes, I promise."

"Anyway, I fly up here to spend time with you and everything's great. The water is clean, the air is fresh, and there were no males clambering to get into my cave. And then, out of nowhere, I find a male who doesn't even want me, and it only makes me want him more."

"So, just to be clear, we're talking about—" Sparu slowly teased out.

Maggie looked down and sighed. "Seamus. Yes, Seamus."

"He is quite the dragon," Sparu conceded, taking another sip. "If I weren't married already, I'd let him take me up to that tower of his and show me how bright his light can get."

Maggie, having been unfortunate enough to have taken a sip of her mimosa just as Sparu began to speak, spit out a cone of boozy orange juice droplets beside her. The couple at the adjacent table glared over at her in disgust. Wiping her mouth with the one-thousand thread count Egyptian cotton napkin, she hastily threw them an apologetic wave.

"You are the worst!" she hissed at her brunch mate. "You are so horny."

Sparu scoffed. "Says the dragon who was just—"

"Shhh," Maggie blurted, this time, to the relief of her friend, finally laughing. "Okay, you got me. It's true, I'm a giant hornball. It had been years since I had mated thanks to that sack of scales I'd been bonded to. So, when I hooked up with Andre a few weeks ago, it rekindled this passion within me."

"Go on," Sparu said, sipping more mimosa between her toothy grin.

"It almost felt like my promethium glands had lit for the first time, you know? Have you ever breathed fire while doing it?"

"Ugh! Only once," Sparu moaned, slumping into her chair at the mention of the act while the memory rushed to the forefront of her brain. "One time after we had just been married, before we had whelps, obviously, we were really going at it. The mood was right, his scales were rubbing just the way I like it, and BAM! It happened. I dang near burned down the tapestries hanging on our kitchen wall."

"The kitchen?!" Maggie exclaimed, smiling coyly.

Sparu grinned, thinking back on that night. "Like I said, the mood was right."

"Anyway, I almost did the other night with Andre," Maggie continued. "We were making out like wild animals. Our jaws were gnashed together, teeth intertwined, and we were just going nuts on each other. I was almost afraid that he'd bite my tongue off in the process. And heck, I would have probably been okay with it in the moment, you know?"

"Mmmhmmm."

"Now, he didn't, thankfully," Maggie said. "And, unfortunately, I didn't breathe fire, either. Granted, that's probably all the better for the resale value of your property, but Tiamat, I would have loved to go that far with him."

Maggie looked back down at the menu for a spell. Sparu could tell that she wasn't reading anything but had simply needed a moment to take a deep breath and get herself back on center.

"When I awoke the next morning, I opened my eyes just in time to watch him walk out the door. Part of me was mad that he would just leave like that without saying goodbye, but in reality, there was no love there. The whole thing was drive by pure lust. Our time together was a simple roll in the sheets for two dragons looking to get laid. I wanted to be ashamed of myself, but I didn't feel any shame whatsoever. That is, until I opened the door."

"What happened?" Sparu ask, now curious. She knew

that there was a Seamus connection here but hadn't seen where the bread crumb trail led off to at this point.

"Well, like a sad little puppy, I walked to the door wrapped in a blank and opened it to watch Andre leave," Maggie began. "I guess that I thought that he'd look back to see me one last time, perhaps regret leaving me in the wee hours of the morning without at least staying for breakfast. But no, he left without a look over his shoulder. When I turned to walk back inside, I realized that Seamus had been standing there the whole time, watching Andre leave first with me close behind."

"So, he knows that you hooked up with Andre?"

"Yeah."

"And that bothers you because—"

"It bothers me," Maggie said, her voice dropping to a whisper, "because I can't stop thinking about Seamus. I can't get him out of my head. We had a moment out in the woods while hunting a few weeks ago, and I thought that something might happen then and there, and if not, at some point soon after. But no, nothing came of it. He's still hung up on his wife and I was too chickenshit to do anything about it at the time."

Maggie paused, biting her lip.

"Well, I tried. But he wasn't fully conscious, and it felt wrong."

Sparu stared at the female from across the table, clearly having more questions than answers by now.

"Not fully conscious?"

"Ugh, it's a long story," Maggie said, exasperatedly. "But long story short, we didn't hook up, let alone convey any form of romantic expression."

"Tiamat, you are a complicated dragon."

"Tell me about it."

"So, what are you going to do?" Sparu asked.

"I don't know," Maggie conceded after a long pause. "I came out here to get away from complications. I thought that I was leaving romantic troubles behind and trading them in for fresh air and good seafood. It was never my intention to fall for another guy, at least not so quickly."

"You're falling for him?"

"I guess so," Maggie admitted. "I haven't felt like this since we were teens. I remember flying out of the cave when my mother wasn't looking to stare at the cute males fly around. I went from not caring about the opposite sex to thinking nothing but of them in a flash. When I'm with Seamus, I feel… I don't know, I just feel like me again. I believe that I could really fall in love once more and actually live side by side in a mutually respectful relationship with another likeminded being. He seems like he would like me for me, and not be intimidated by a strong, successful female who doesn't need a male to take care of her."

"I don't know, it's kind of nice, sometimes," Sparu added. "Sometimes I pretend that I can't reach a jar off a high shelf and ask my husband to grab it for me. It makes him happy, even though he knows that I could probably stretch a little harder, use a chair, or heck, you know, fly up to the shelf."

"Don't get me wrong, it would be nice on occasion," Maggie said. "But it was definitely something that stood between me and my ex-bondmate. He was literally offended when I'd refuse his help with something and took any of my independence or self-reliance as a personal attack on him. I'm not saying that it was the reason we ultimately drifted apart, but it certainly didn't help."

Sparu took another sip, followed by a very long, very deep breath before answering.

"Well, you know that Seamus isn't available, right? And may not be for the foreseeable future?"

"Yeah."

"And trust me," Sparu continued. "I've watched a few aspiring females take a run at him over the past few years. They couldn't get him to flinch. It's nothing personal to you, he's just not ready and won't be until he sorts things out. That could be another month, it could be another decade."

"So, what do you think that I should do?"

"If I were in your shoes? You want me to be honest?"

"Please!" Maggie pleaded, lowering her voice as she caught a few nearby dragons staring in her direction.

"I would do one of two things," Sparu began, holding up a single claw on each hand. "One, you can go back to the bungalow and keep playing with your shower wand, electric toothbrush, or whatever other sorts of toys you may have hidden away."

Maggie blushed and shot her a look.

"And I'm not saying that there's anything wrong with that!" Sparu spat back, eagerly. "I've been known to press the starter button on the ole engine every once in a while, if you know what I mean."

Maggie stuck her tongue out at her friend, cutting the tension between them and dimming the reddish hue of the scales on her face.

"And the second?"

"Or two, you can stick your tail back out there and try a few more dates."

Sparu could see Maggie already getting flustered and

ready to defend herself.

"Slow down, slow down!" she said. "I know that the first attempt left you feeling down, and it then potentially messed things up with Seamus. But, there are a lot of good looking, single dragons in the area who would love to shack up with a female such as yourself."

"I'm not looking to 'shack up' with anyone," Maggie said.

"You know what I mean," Sparu returned, looking at her caringly. "I'm just saying that there is a vibrant dating scene around here, especially now that the weather is nicer, and you're a good catch for whatever lucky dragons comes your way."

"Fine," Maggie said, letting out a breath she didn't realize she'd been holding in. "I don't even know where to begin, though. Do you know any gents looking for a sassy gal like me?"

"I know a few, but I think that I can lend a hand," Sparu said, trying to reassure her. "I can think of a few males who might be worthy to date my bestie, and I'll pick Claudio's brain about some guys who he may know. Plus, there's this."

Sparu pulled her phone out from under the table where she had been surreptitiously punching away at the screen. She turned it around and handed it to Maggie screen-first. Maggie took the device and looked down at the open app.

"A dating site? I'm not doing online dating."

"Oh, get over yourself, Maggie. It's the future. It's how the younglings are all finding their broodmates nowadays. Unless you want to date a bunch of old fogie dragons who post personal ads on microfiche, you might as well embrace modern technology and get out there."

"Ugh, I hate you."

"You're welcome," Sparu answered, smiling. "And, I love you, too."

Chapter XIII

"I can't believe that I'm really doing this," Maggie said out loud, more for her own benefit than to necessarily let Sparu know how silly she thought this whole affair was. "Seriously, though. Hatch dot com? Who the hell comes up with this stuff?"

"It's supposed to be the best… for dragons like you," Sparu said, turning away.

"Dragons like me. Meaning—"

"—dragons, you know, dragons who shop at DressCave."

Sparu ducked as a pillow zipped through the space which her head had formerly occupied. The pillow was followed by a whip of a tail and easily blocked by the recipient. She knew that Maggie understood the zing, but it was still hard to admit that you may be beyond the peak of your life's flight through the sky of time.

"Okay! Okay, cease fire," Sparu said, laughing as Maggie wound back for another whip. "You know what I mean. It's a dating website designed for single adults with grown children. It's supposed to be really good!"

"But it's so corny!" Maggie blurted out. "Just look at the tagline: Hatch.com, an Eggcellent Future Awaits! Like, I get that they're playing off the whole theme of me having laid eggs, cared for the occupants, and then watched them leave me to my terrible marriage while feeling barren and alone, but come on. It's just a little on the nose."

"Well, we could try some of the other options if you like," Sparu said, giving her a wink. "Maybe TiamatMingle? Flamr? PlentyOfDragons? Ooh! You could try Dragon Friend Finder if you just want to hook up with hot singles in your area."

Sparu kept reading through the list on her computer screen, chuckling as she went on. She was obviously enjoying this far more than Maggie.

"Some of these names are really awesome," Sparu said. "You should try some of these just to see what kind of weirdos sign up."

"You mean, like me?"

"No!" Sparu shot back. "You're hot stuff, Hun. You're liquified promethium, babe. Any dragon on these sites would be honored to share a cave with you for a night."

"I'm not looking to share a cave for a night, and you know it," Maggie said, giving her friend a stern look. It was clear that the jokes had gone far enough, and it was time to get serious.

"Roger that," Sparu said, giving her a sarcastic salute. "I'm sorry. Back to business. What will it be then? Want to try one of these, hit the pub scene, or something in between?"

"Ugh! I hate trying to talk to dragons at the pub, at least trying to meet them," Maggie said, exhaling loudly. "This is so lame. Let's do this and get it over with."

Looking back to her screen, Maggie punched in her payment information and created an account. And thus, the profile for MagDestroyer1982 was born.

Sitting at a table in the back corner of the Old Flames, Maggie looked down at her phone for the dozenth time in so many minutes. She was meeting another dragon for drinks tonight and was nervous. The male was now twenty minutes late and she felt compelled to just up and leave, but she kind of liked this one and had hoped that things would work out between them.

It had been a long process thus far. Two months had passed since she'd agreed to try online dating at Sparu's encouragement and there was little to show for it. Granted, there had been some nice moments with a few of the gentledragons, but she had mostly wound up with a bunch of really great stories to share with Sparu afterwards over a few flagons of wine. Yet, date after failed date, she had nothing so far that would actually bring her long-term happiness in a committed relationship.

"Excuse me, miss?"

Maggie looked up to see Claudio standing before her, holding an extremely delicate, human-made drinking glass in his claws. He was carefully pinching it by the stem with one clawed hand while holding it by the bottom with the other on top of a napkin.

"Oh, Claudio!" Maggie exclaimed, happy to see her old friend. "How are you doing? I didn't know that you were working tonight. Please, sit."

She motioned for the male to take a seat across from her. While they had been relatively unacquainted before, only knowing each other through Sparu, they had grown closer over the past few months. For safety reasons, Sparu had encouraged Maggie to meet most of her dates at the Old Flames just so that Claudio could keep an eye on her in case something went wrong. Maggie, of course, had protested against it, saying that she could take care of herself. But, the other two dragons had strongly urged that she take them up on the offer, and she had ultimately given in. Claudio had grown to see Maggie like a daughter and couldn't bear the thought of some dinosaur-brained belly-dragger hurting her.

The dragon gently set the glass down before her and pulled out the unused chair. Sitting down, he leaned back and let out a small sigh. It had been a busy night at the pub, and from what Maggie could tell, all of the employees had been running around like cattle with their heads bitten off just trying to keep up. She set her phone down on the table along with her keys and pushed them off to the right to make more room for the other dragon.

"Things are going quite well, my lass, quite well," Claudio answered after finally settling himself down in the old wooden chair. "Thank you for asking. But the real question is, how are you doing? I know that I've seen you in here with a lot of gentledragons lately, but rarely have I seen you this glum."

"A lot?" Maggie shot back. "Claudio, you make me sound like a harlot."

He blushed at the accusation and laughed. He meant no ill will toward her with the statement and was merely reflecting on her recent history.

"You know what I mean. I'm just saying that you've been doing a good job of staying open minded and mixing it up with the single dragons of Bar Harbor," he said, holding his hands up in mock defense. "And so far, you've seemed to be having a good time, albeit unsuccessful in your endeavors. And tonight, you seem sad before the date has even begun. Is everything alright?"

Maggie looked down at the table, fidgeting with her claws. She was half-pretending to focus on scraping a rough spot on one claw by scratching with another, but both of the dragons knew that she was just avoiding the subject. She looked up into the older man's eyes and sighed, slumping back into her chair.

"Well, I was having a good time, until I realized that I was my own worst enemy."

"How so?"

"After the fifth or sixth date at this very table, it occurred to me that all of these dragons, well, most of them, at least, we're really nice guys," she began, pausing every few words as if she were having difficulty piecing the words together. "But by the end of each date, things would go sour and we'd both walk away agreeing that it was nice to meet, but that we weren't a good match."

Claudio nodded and continued to listen, giving her all the time to speak. He had heard enough stories of love, lust, and heartbreak to know that there was more to this story. She took the cue and kept going.

"Each time, I'd leave and mope the whole way back to my bed where I'd proceed to down a tub of ice cream from the freezer. The same ice cream which I would buy the day before the date knowing that I'd need it for afterwards. And you know what I realized through all of this?"

"What's that?"

"That it was all my fault!" she said, throwing her claws

out wide as she stood up, knocking a saltshaker to the ground and pushing the chair backwards. "There was nothing wrong with them and there was only one consistent variable in all of these failed equations! It was me! It was me all this time. I have been self-sabotaging every single one of my dates since I've been here, and they've all crashed and burned having been doomed to failure from the start."

She dropped back to her chair, the wood creaking in protest. She wasn't a heavy dragon by any definition of the word, but even strong wooden frames had a hard time putting up with frustrated dragons at the end of their wits. Maggie caught her breath from the tirade while Claudio leaned, pondering her words.

Leaning forward after a spell, he opened his mouth as if to speak but paused. Reaching out, he snatched up her wine glass and sipped a long pull of the sweet grape juice. Maggie shot him a look.

"Calm down," he said, holding one hand up to quell her fury before it began. "I'll get you another glass, don't worry."

She harrumphed.

"It is good wine," he conceded. "I picked that up for a song down in Kittery. You wouldn't believe how much those humans will shave off their asking price once you start fuming a little smoke out of your nostrils."

Maggie rolled her eyes.

"Alright, sorry," he said. "Where was I? Right. So, have you told him how you feel?"

Maggie's brain stopped dead in its tracks. She hadn't been expecting such a straightforward question from Claudio and had been hoping to just use him as an echo chamber to vent her angst and frustration, with little to show for it afterwards other than having felt listened to. But woah. He was right, and she wasn't sure if she had even admitted it to herself yet.

"Told who?" She replied, purposely being coy. She knew that he knew and was a little embarrassed by how clearly she could be read. But she wanted to hear him say it out loud.

Claudio merely looked back at her down the length of his snout. She looked away, slowly returning her eyes to his after a moment of ponderance.

"I tried," she conceded. "Really, I did! And I thought that there was something there, that he may have felt the same. It wasn't meant to be, though. He still loves his wife and will until the day she returns, or he dies, whichever comes first."

Claudio shook his head, the sorrow evident upon his scale-lined eyes. "He is a sad sort to watch slumping around this town. Everyone knows that the lass isn't coming back, it's just been too long. But their love won't falter until one of them draws their last breath and the other has their chance to see them off."

Maggie looked down at her phone as she heard a chime come from it. She could see a message pop up:

I just landed outside the pub and I'm on my way in. I am SO sorry!

"Well, that's my cue, miss" Claudio said, standing back up. He pulled the chair out a little further and tidied up the place setting, making it show-ready for the dragon about to arrive. "I'll give you two a few minutes and come over with some menus."

"Thank you, Claudio," Maggie replied. "And thank

you for listening."

The dragon gave a slight bow and walked back to the bar. He would normally try to make any of his patrons happy, but he had decided long ago to take Maggie under his wing.

A moment later, Maggie's date walked in, face sweaty and flustered from the frantic flight. He explained that he had been caught up at work and lost track of time. She understood and forgave him with a laugh, but she couldn't really care any less. Maggie wasn't thinking about him, his job, or why he had been late.

Later that evening after a non-exciting, fairly mundane dinner, Maggie and her date agreed to call it a night. He had tried to pay for the entire meal, but Maggie insisted that they split the check. He held the door for her as they left the Old Flames and she accepted, but that would be the end of things. She felt no connection to the male and didn't want to lead him on any further but didn't want to appear off-putting. It was exhausting trying to make everyone happy and not offend them. But, alas, that was the life of a single female dragon trying to make her way in this world. You seem too eager and you're a slut; not eager enough, and you're a bitch. Go figure.

As she walked down the front steps leading into the pub, Maggie saw a group of dragons making their way down the sidewalk toward the entrance. Stepping off to the side to make room for the incoming patrons, she saw a lone figure entering with them a few wingspans back.

It was Seamus.

Walking toward the Old Flames, he noticed Maggie standing there. Despite the sour expression on her face as she tried to look away from him before he could have a chance to recognize her, she looked resplendent. She had dressed up, wore her finest jewelry, and had even spritzed on some human-made perfume for the date. Not able to resist a glance for long, she looked up and noticed Seamus checking her out. He was clearly trying not to be obvious about it, but a lady could always tell.

Walking up to her, his mouth opened to say something when the dragon holding the door for the incoming group approached. The male walked up to Maggie and stood next to her.

"Woah, all those dragons and not one single tip!" the dragon joked, looking to Maggie. He put a clawed hand behind her and rested on the ridge spikes of the small of her back. She moved away, looking awkwardly to Seamus. "Maggie, who's your friend?"

Seamus' face hardened, and any glimmer of attraction, happiness, or fondness of chancing to see her again in this brief encounter fizzled away. He stood up straight and nodded to her as he slipped by them and entered the pub.

CHAPTER XIV

R O O A A R R R

Incorrect.

R O O O A A R R

Incorrect.

R O A O A R R R

Incorrect.

"Ah!" Maggie yelled out, drawing the attention of those nearby patrons in the pub. She was in the front corner of Old Flames enjoying a delightful little brunch by the window. Claudio had never opened this early in the past, but at the suggestion of Maggie and Sparu to start slinging fancy crepes to attract more of the human customers, he had finally caved. And to good results.

Which was quite contrary to Maggie's game this morning. Her continued outbursts eventually drew the attention of the proprietor himself who shuffled over with a pitcher of orange juice. Dropping into the chair next to her, he grabbed her glass and gave her a refill, to which she thanked him by leaning over and resting her head on his shoulder.

"This game is so dumb," she muttered while tapping in another string of characters.

"What's that, my lass?" Claudio asked, looking down at her phone. "Is this one of those mobile games I hear you kids going on about?"

His use of the word kids made the female snort, spitting out a freshly sipped mouthful of OJ through her pointy teeth. While she was definitely younger than Claudio, he wasn't that old that he shouldn't be familiar with how smartphones worked.

"Yes, it is, gramps," she said, raising her head and elbowing him in the side. "It's a new game called Roardle that our dear pain-in-the-ass friend, Sparu, got me hooked on. Every morning a new clue pops up which describes a scenario where you'd roar at something. You then need to phonetically spell the sound of the roar based on the clue, using only eight letters.

Curious, the older dragon squinted down at the illuminated screen and read the clue for that day.

Stepping on a LEGO and then dropping your flagon of coffee on your toe.

"Oh! That's an easy one," he said. "It's got to be Roaaaarr. Try that."

Grinning at his quick answer which surely must be correct, she enthusiastically took the phone back from him and punched in the characters.

R O A A A A R R

Incorrect.

"Dammit," he muttered. "Well, I gave it my best shot. Good luck, my dear."

Sticking her tongue out at him as he stood and walked back to the bar, Maggie turned the screen off and placed the phone down on the table. Tipping the bottom of her flagon to the ceiling, she downed the last of the juice and collected her things. Tossing a few coins down next to the plates, she waved to the locals whom she knew and headed for the door.

Stopping at the bulletin board next to the entrance, she noticed a new ad which hadn't been there upon entering. It was offering sailing lessons in the harbor and had precut tabs dangling at the bottom with the instructor's contact information. Turning her head to the side, she read the name but didn't recognize the dragon.

"Hey Claudio," she yelled back toward her friend at the bar, ripping one of the perforated tabs off the page. "Do you know who this is?"

"Aye, that's me, lass," a human voice called out from a few tables over before Claudio could answer.

Maggie turned her head toward the source of the words and froze. It took all her willpower to stop from laughing at how obnoxiously stereotypical this man appeared. He sat there on one of the rare smaller stools in the shadows of a corner away from the windows.

The boat captain had one foot perched on an adjacent chair, while the other foot, a prosthetic wooden leg, sat resting on the floor. He was wearing a blue-grey turtleneck sweater underneath a dark blue peacoat, and a white service cap rested upon a billowing collection of curly gray hair.

Walking over toward his table, she greeted the human and thanked him for the quick response. She was thinking of calling the number on the slip immediately upon reading it, so this was perfect timing. He motioned for her to pull up a seat, so she scooted an empty dragon-sized chair over to the table and joined him.

"My name is Rexforth Bradley Baker, but you can call me Captain Rex," the man said, offering his hand to Maggie.

Maggie, stunned by the motion, paused for a moment before gingerly accepting and shaking hands. Due to the size different between the two species, it was often cumbersome, and downright dangerous, for dragons and humans to share some of their bodily traditions. She had heard stories of dragons crushing human arms trying to shake hands, give high-fives, and other forms of greeting. Most of her species opted to simply bow or nod their head in this instance, but she couldn't refuse the generous act. For him to offer his hand like this, he must be very brave or implicitly trust her. Either way, he went up a few notches in her book.

"I am the captain of my ship, the Tranquility," the man continued after their shake. His voice belied a modicum of a wince, which was impressive to Maggie given their hardy clasp. "The ship is a larger craft, about two of your wingspans in length, and originally built as a human luxury craft. It is sail powered with an auxiliary motor for backup and has been stripped down to make more room for dragons on the main deck."

The man took a puff from his pipe and set it down, turning away from Maggie before blowing the smoke out. The musky plume didn't bother her, for obvious reasons, but she still appreciated the effort. She knew that not all humans tolerated tobacco smoke, let alone any smoke at all, and recognized that his action was one of respect toward her.

"My apologies, miss," the captain said, tapping the pipe into an ashtray set upon the tabletop. It was a bit rough out there today and this helps settle my nerves. Even after all these years at sea, it can still shake you up pretty good."

Maggie nodded in agreement while a small voice in the back of her head told her to be worried. If this hardened, grizzled man could get scared sailing along these coasts, why in her right mind would she go out there?

"So, tell me," he continued, taking another puff from the wooden pipe. "What is a young lady such as yourself looking to do with sailing lessons? Is it for a human friend of yours?"

"They're for me!" she answered, the excited tones jumping from her throat. "I had a boyfriend years ago who used to sail, and I really enjoyed it. I haven't been out on the water since we broke up though and thought that it'd be fun to get back out there."

"A sailor, huh?" the man bellowed, slapping his knee. "You don't look like the type of gal who likes seamen."

The sound of a glass shattering behind her echoed throughout the relatively quiet pub. Maggie turned around to see Claudio at the bar, a drying towel in his hand, slapping the bar top. He was biting his other hand in a vain attempt to calm his laughter. He gave up and bellowed a lout hoot, finally calming himself and bending down to begin collecting the broken shards of glass on the floor.

Maggie rolled her eyes at him and turned back to Captain Rex.

"Don't mind him," she said. "Male dragons mature at a later age than females."

"Was it something that I said?"

More laughter rose from the bar, but quickly stopped as Maggie whipped her head around to stare lasers into Claudio's thick skull. He took the hint and clammed up, slowly lowering himself below the bar and out of her view.

As if that would stop her flames from finding him.

"No," she said, shaking her head. "But yes, I had a thing for sea going gents in my younger years and was quite smitten with the sailor."

The captain stood up a little straighter in his chair and gave her a wink. This elicited a giggle from Maggie.

"*Dragon* sailors," she said slyly to the old man. "No offense."

The older man laughed, slapping his knee. "None taken, lass."

"Anyway, I ended up loving the ocean more than him by the end of our relationship. I've yet to sail again since those days but have always had a special place in my heart for the deep blue waters of the Atlantic."

"Well, you've convinced me, my dear," the captain said. "I'm on the water every day, so you can begin whenever you like."

"What are you doing tomorrow?"

"Aha!" Captain Rex yelled over the wind. "You've almost got it now, Maggie! Change tack to get us windward on the starboard side."

Maggie worked the lines, adjusting the angle of the boom while pulling hard on the tiller. Feeling the boat starting to lean as expected, she swung herself to the other side of the ship. The boat continued to lean away from the wind as the mainsail billowed out, catching more of the wind and driving them forward.

"You've got it, my dear!" Rexforth jumped across

the deck, grabbing hold of one of the stanchions supporting the lifeline running along the perimeter of the boat. Wedging his feet against the inside of the hull, he braced himself. "We're heeling now! Woah! Look at that lean. Haha!"

The old man yelled into the wind, loving every minute of this. Maggie on the other hand, even after having done this multiple times in the last three weeks, would have pissed her pants had she been wearing any. Some human phrases didn't necessarily translate well over to dragonkind.

"Ah!" she screamed, looking back over her shoulder. Through her wings rippling behind her, she could barely see the water below them as the hull continued to tilt away from the wind. Maggie looked straight down past her feet to the port side of the boat, which was practically in the water by now, and felt her stomach rise into her throat at the sight of the waves racing by. Foaming crests crashed over the edge of the ship, spilling water onto the deck with each pulsing throw from the ocean. "We're going to flip!"

"Nay, my lass! The keel is good and strong. She won't let us down today!"

Maggie gulped at his words, unable to vocally respond. While she was a fairly smart dragon and understood the principles of keel design and ballast placement within a modern boat, she still found it difficult to believe, let alone trust it, at times like this. The captain had done a good job pushing the dragon to her limits and finding out where her comfort zone was. He'd bring her just to that point during their lessons, force her to tiptoe past the line, and then calmly bring her back into known territory. She absolutely hated him for it but steadily became a better sailor with each passing lesson. It was hard to admit, but the old salty dog knew his stuff.

Riding up and down on the large waves coming into the harbor from the ocean, Maggie was being thrown up and down off the edge of the deck. She gritted her teeth as the hard deck material slammed into her butt over and over again, wincing at the pain and knowing that she'd have a bruise there in the morning. Apparently, she was out of practice back there.

Gripping on to the lifeline and hooking her toes under a part of the cabin, she steadied herself to the boat and tried to ride the waves with it. If there was one thing which she had learned from the past few weeks of sailing, it was that the ocean was amazingly powerful, unrelenting, and didn't give two craps about what you thought. If you wanted to go out and try to navigate her waters in a tiny boat instead of just flying through the air like Tiamat intended, then you checked your demands at the cave opening and submitted. The ocean wasn't necessarily something to be feared, but it did require your respect.

Looking down at the tiny human next to her, she smiled at the sheer joy emblazoned upon his face. Even after all these years of commanding vessels out on the open water, the man still found excitement in a tiny ride around the Mt. Desert Narrows. Granted, he was probably finding most of his enjoyment in watching a dragon flailing around in his boat, being thrown around by comparatively miniscule waves, but it was still nice. She loved it out on the water, even if she had spent most of her life merely flying over the crests of the waves as she soared past.

Focusing back on the bow of the craft, she pulled on the tiller until the edge of Bean Island crept around and off to starboard. They had looped around the island and were on their return trip back to Bar Harbor. The captain wasn't based out of Bar Harbor, hailing from his home port of Sorrento Harbor, but Maggie met him at the municipal pier for their lessons. She had offered to fly out and meet him at his dock, but he sternly refused. He loved these waters and relished in the time he spent by himself sailing out to meet her.

With the island slipping past them off to the right, she adjusted her tack and aimed for the southwest. The bow swung around and pointed her way back to Bar Harbor to bring her home. It was a funny feeling of home. She had never thought that she'd stay long enough to get comfortable around here, but after several months and experiencing several of the cooler Maine seasons, the place was growing on her.

Shifting the boom, she caught the wind with the mainsail, obscuring her view of most of the land off to starboard. She could see the tip of Hancock Point enough to know that she was out to sea and away from the shallow waters surrounding the peninsula but couldn't see much beyond that. Which is why she felt so confused when she saw Captain Rex waving wildly as they passed.

"Who are you waving to?" she called out.

"My friend over there!" he yelled back, struggling to speak over the wind rushing inland from the Atlantic over their exposed backs. "He runs the lighthouse out in the middle of the Narrows."

Maggie stared down at the man, perplexed. She wasn't aware of any lighthouse in the water nearby, but probably should by now. The captain had urged her to memorize the maps of the area before setting out and she had admittedly tried, but there was so much to learn, and she felt like she was drinking from a fire hose. Maggie scolded herself for not knowing and made a promise to learn all the key points tonight when she sat down to study with a glass of wine.

Pulling on the tiller to bring the bow more southward, she froze. A conversation from many months past came to the forefront of her mind and slapped her in the face, waking her to the realization that she did know of a lighthouse over there. Stretching her neck upward and scooting her butt aftward to see around the mainsail, a small structure jutting up from the dark blue waters finally entered her vision. There, waving back to Captain Rexforth, was the lighthouse keeper himself. A tall, red dragon with mighty wings wrapped around its body like a cloak, stood there watching the craft slip through the choppy waters. Recognizing his friend down on the stern of the ship, the dragon pulled back its right wing to wave a clawed hand down at the passersby.

Against her better judgement, and the advice of nearly every sailing book she had recently read, Maggie stood up on the deck, struggling to balance herself throughout the process. The boat rocked with the rapidly changing center of gravity, and she dug her claws into the painted white wood of the tall, erect mast before her. Leaning forward, adding to the already strong tilt of the craft, she pushed the boat and herself further leeward. She could hear Captain Rex hoot and holler across from her, but she paid him no mind. Maggie suddenly forgot everything else going on about her and tunnel visioned in on the keeper atop his home.

Seamus. It was Seamus waving down to them, and he just finally realized that Rexforth had not only a dragon with him onboard, but Maggie.

Seamus paused mid-wave, staring down into Maggie's eyes. Despite the distance between the two, their enhanced vision shortened the gap to what humans would have seen in just a few feet. His eyes bore into hers, and hers into his. Neither dragon made a move and probably would have gone on like this forever had it not been for the mast attacking Maggie.

"Oww!" she screamed over the wind as the hard wood of the mast slammed into her face.

"Get yerself down, lass!" Captain Rex yelled up at her. "The waves are getting bigger, and you need to drop down to the deck. Get your tail back down here and help me heel off on port to keep this thing from flipping."

Maggie, embarrassed, looked back to Seamus and gave him a little wave. He waved back, breaking into a visible chuckle when he could finally see that she was okay. Not able to help herself, she joined in, laughing at her predicament and the shared moment between the two.

Staring back up at him, she silently mouthed the word bye and gave him a final wave. He returned the gesture, paused, and dove from the top of the lighthouse.

Stretching his wings before he fell to the rocky ledge protruding from the waters below, he caught the wind and shot back to the sky. Zipping out in front of the boat, he zigzagged back and forth off to their portside, showing off for Maggie. She watched as he soared over the water and faded into the green blur of the hills of Bar Harbor.

CHAPTER XV

"Maggie, me dear," Captain Rex called out from the deck of the boat. "Toss me those lines, will ya?"

Maggie, up on the floating dock adjacent to the Selkie, Captain Rex's commercial fishing boat, looked down to where he was pointing and gathered up the ten coils of rope. Using a trick she had figured out a few weeks back, she curled her tail to her side, strung her appendage through the center of each coil, and swung it around to the center of the boat. Tipping her tail downward, she slid each one down to the fiberglass surface in a neat little row. The trick got a round of applause from the human patrons onboard today and an appreciative head nod from Rexforth.

The dragon had been on the captain's payroll now for a few months and spent a few hours here and there helping the man out. After picking up the art of sailing fairly quickly during her initial lessons, the man had asked her to stay on with his service and help out when and where needed, especially if she could use a little extra pocket change. While her expenses were more than covered by her maintenance work back at Sparu's campground, the extra coins in her purse would allow her to pick up some nice treats every once in a while. Besides, she liked working with the man and loved her extra time out on the water. And the captain loved having an extremely strong dragon capable of lifting things he could never fathom to help ease the burden on the job.

Loading a few cases of supplies over the side and down to the waiting hands of some of the human crew, Maggie stood up and stretched her back. It wasn't hard work for her, but the constant bending up and down wore on her by the end of the morning. She felt a few of her vertebrae pop into position and shook her arms and legs to loosen up the muscles. Leaning her head back to give her spine one more crack for good measure, she found herself face to face with a red blur.

Before she had time to react, the blur crashed down onto the dock beside her, flinging her and the remaining gear into the air. The floating segments rippled along the length of the dock, gently whipping back and forth as the energy bounced along the connected line back to shore. The sudden motion of the dock pushed and pulled on the water between it and the boat, causing the fifty-foot vessel to bob back and forth. Everyone, whether they wanted to or not, had fallen witness to Seamus being in a playful mood.

Those who had managed to not fall down on their butts, or at least had gotten back up quickly enough, let out a roar of laughter. This wasn't the first time they had seen the dragon pull a similar prank. Those who had not gotten back up so well were still in the process of launching a volley of jokes and mild-mannered insults toward the red behemoth.

"Heh, sorry everyone," Seamus said, failing to hold back a chuckle in their direction. "I saw your new deckhand here and lost track of what I was doing."

Maggie gave him a wink while several of the humans

let out a few whistles. Whereas humans and dragons were still at bitter odds with one another in some parts of the world, they had found ways to bond well enough in places like Bar Harbor. Their mutual love of the ocean, good food, and the clean air and woodlands of the northeast US has acted as a catalyst to bring the two species together and accelerate their societal integration. It wasn't perfect by a longshot, but it was getting closer as time progressed.

Seamus looked down at Maggie, smiling. "Good morning, Miss Maggie."

"Good morning, Seamus," she replied.

She couldn't help smiling back up at him, her eyes shifting to the side when she realized she was staring. They had been bumping into each other more often lately, especially once he realized that she was typically near the docks in the early hours of the day. She had a feeling that he was flying out to town for no reason other than to find her. While she had no proof of his motives, she wasn't about to start complaining.

"What brings you to town this fine morning?"

"Oh, you know," he began, scratching at an itch behind one of his horns. "I needed a loaf of bread, or something, and I figured that I'd take a trip."

"Bread or something?" she quoted back to him, grinning slyly. "You're telling me that there's not a single good baker on all of Hancock Point worth patronizing this morning? You had to fly all the way down here for some freshly baked bread?"

"Hancock Point? Please. Those yuppies don't own an oven and you know it."

"Hey!" One of the human fishermen yelled up from the boat. "I'm from The Point!"

Maggie turned back to face Seamus, putting a claw up to her mouth to stave off her laughter. He leaned in, almost touching nose-to-nose. They both snickered, desperately holding back their laughter at the commentary between dragon and human while trying not to sound too obvious in front of the sailors. Composing herself, she turned back to the boat full of crusty old men and wannabe human sailors.

"Captain!" Maggie called out. "Are you good here if I take off?"

"Aye, me lass, aye," he hollered back. Looking to Seamus standing next to her, he added in, "And take your time. We'll have this under control in no time. We'll be seeing ya tomorrow!"

Maggie waved them off before turning back to Seamus. He nodded his head toward the shore and stuck out his left elbow. Glancing down at the protruding joint and back to his face, she felt her blood pressure spike as her heart revved up a few extra beats per minute. Blood rushed through her veins and warmed her face to the point where she knew that she was blushing. Reaching out with her right claw, she was about to slip her hand through his arm when they heard the horn blare.

Turning back toward the water, the two dragons scanned the fog-ridden harbor. They could only see the faint outline of a craft coming through the water, only fully emerging just before it was upon them. Jumping back, Maggie grabbed onto Seamus' muscled limb to steady herself as the fifty-footer bumped into the tires on the side of the dock, coming to a slow stop.

"Uhh! Sorry!" the human at the helm called out, realizing that he had brought the craft in a little too fast.

Even from here, the two dragons could see that something was wrong by the expression on his face. The tone of his voice hinted at more to come.

A human deckhand approached the edge of the new ship's lifeline, about to heave a coiled line over the edge to Seamus. He paused, obviously not realizing at first that there were two massive dragons standing there before him, but ultimately let the rope fly. Seamus caught it with ease and deftly tied a cleat hitch knot to hold the vessel in place. Another of the human crew members jumped onto the deck, tying another line to a second cleat at the other end of the boat to secure it.

Not one to pass up a curious incident, Captain Rex climbed up onto the dock to poke around and see what was going on. From his vantage point down on the Selkie, he could see that the humans were uncomfortable around Seamus and Maggie. He figured that if he intervened, he could probably get more info out of them than his two friends. He gave Seamus a look and the dragon stepped back a wingspan, clearly sensing his plan.

"Ahoy there," he called out to the nearest human from the newly arrived vessel. "My name is Rexforth, captain of the Selkie, here. You guys seem a little flustered. Is everything okay?

A second crewmember walked up next to the first, and both looked quickly between Captain Rex and the two nearby dragons. They didn't exactly seem afraid of them, but there was clearly something on their mind that they were nervous about discussing… or there was something on the boat they were afraid to show.

The first man gulped, trying to steady himself on the still shaking dock and prepare for the talk. He looked again at Seamus specifically, then back to Rexforth.

"I, um, I'm Noah, captain of the Loch Hunter, here," the man began. His eyes kept shifting back to Seamus, who was becoming visibly annoyed with each passing glance. "We were fishing in the waters east of here, close to Nova Scotia, when we came upon a small island."

He shifted his feet, his eyes wandering about, looking at anything and everything aside from the eyes of the dragons and humans on the dock.

"It wasn't on our maps and looked like a nice place to check out, so we took our inflatable over to take a look," he continued. "We were on the island for all of five minutes when we came upon a roughly built shelter hidden amongst a copse of trees. As soon as we got close, this mad dragon came thundering out trying to claw at us. It lunged at my first mate here and almost took a bite out of him. But one quick hit with a stick knocked it out."

Rexforth looked over to Seamus and Maggie who were growing increasingly uncomfortable with the story. He could tell that they didn't like the usage of the words 'mad' or 'it'. Humans often referred to dragons as simple beasts or creatures and deprived them of more humanized nomenclature only reserved for their own kind. Granted, dragons could be just as harsh towards humans, so it was far from being an equal world where both species respected the other.

"After the initial shock wore off, we inspected the shelter and realized that it must have been a shipwreck survivor," Noah explained. "Between materials used on the shelter having been clearly salvaged from a boat, the damaged wings on the beast, and its malnourished state, we could tell that the thing must have washed up years ago after a rough time out at sea. We have tried talking to the creature during its brief moments of consciousness, but it doesn't understand English and just keeps roaring at us."

Growing agitated, Seamus finally stepped forward. "Is it a female?" he whispered, barely loud enough to be heard by anyone further than a wingspan away. "Is it, my…"

"Let me take a look, son, alright?" Captain Rex broke in. He knew where Seamus was going with this and couldn't bear to see him suffer further. He had known his wife before she disappeared and would be able to quickly answer the dragon's mystery.

Seamus nodded, conceding to the man's request. He figured that the humans wouldn't want another dragon onboard Loch Hunter and that he would only negatively add to the situation.

"Do ye mind, lad?" Rexforth asked Noah, giving a nod toward the hold of the ship.

The man nodded in assent, moving aside to let the captain pass. Jumping down to the deck of the ship, Rex steadied himself and walked over to the hold. Looking down into the opening, he was finally able to see the dragon inside. Creeping through the opening, the older man carefully sniffed the hold and the dragon, looking for anything which may be amiss. After a few minutes, he reemerged from the dark enclosure and returned back to the group on the dock.

"It's not her, Seamus," Rexforth said, with a gentle nod. He could tell by the other's reaction that Seamus was both relieved and saddened. He didn't want her to be dead but finding out what had actually happened and receiving an ounce of closure over the incident would have been a blessing. "It's some male whom I've never seen before.

But, he's unconscious and needs your help."

Turning back to the other humans, the captain crouched down to address them.

"My thanks in returning this boy," he began, directly addressing Noah. "But he needs medical care that only their kind can provide. Do you mind if we board and take him away from here to a dragon hospital?"

"By all means," Noah said, motioning to the ship with his hands. "I have a boom winch if that helps to life him up and out of there."

"No need, lad. Thank you all the same."

Nodding to Rexforth, Seamus and Maggie leapt into the air and gingerly alighted onto the upper deck. Crouching low, they both reached in and grabbed the male by his arms and legs. Gently gripping the four appendages, and careful to avoid contact with the improperly healed wing remnants, they flew over to the dock with him. They hovered slowly to the surface of the deck, tenderly placing the male on his back.

Seamus, thanking Rexforth for his help and nodding in thanks to the humans for their rescue, turned to Maggie.

"Maggie, this is Wilhelm, one of…" he began, choking up halfway through. "One of Matilda's crew members. I need to get him to the hospital. Please fly ahead to alert the doctors and I'll meet you there."

Maggie stared back at Seamus, unable to speak. She didn't know what to say, even if she could. Without a second thought, she pushed off from the dock and took to the air, flying straight toward the center of town to where the primary dragon hospital was located.

Seamus bent back to the dock and looked the man up and down. He had known Wilhelm only through Matilda and her tales of life out on the sea but had been a good worker from all accounts.

Matilda.

The name rang hollow in his hears. Not a day has passed where he hadn't thought of her, but it had been years since he said her name out loud. The sound of it resonated oddly in his ears, like something so intimately familiar yet distantly foreign. Wilhelm's arrival, though completely unexpected after all this time, brought renewed hope to Seamus' spirits. At the very least, the male now knew where to resume his search for his beloved wife. At the worst, he may very well find out her ultimate fate from this male upon his awakening.

Dropping to his knees, he scooped the dragon up in his massive arms, adjusting the male's body to compensate for the increased mass during flight. Feeling confident in his hold, he gave a final nod to Rexforth and the others before pushing off from the dock. Mighty wings pumping the air, he struggled at first but finally took to the sky. Gaining speed, he pointed himself toward the hospital and put on as much power as he could muster.

Several days later, Seamus and Maggie were seated outside the male's room at Bar Harbor General Hospital. They had been allowed to sit with him in his room as they were the closest thing the dragon had to family at this point but had ventured out after the first twenty-four hours to make more room for the doctors. As he wasn't awake yet and they had little to no professional medical knowledge, there was little that they could do for the dragon.

Opening her eyes, Maggie glanced around the hallway, still groggy and confused as to where they were and why. Her head was sideways and resting on something. Slowly straightening in her chair, she tried not to wake Seamus as her head lifted from his shoulder. She recalled sitting with him in these chairs late last night but couldn't recall drifting off. Had they both fallen asleep together and he didn't know? Or had she fallen asleep first, laying her head onto him, and if so, what had he thought about it?

These thoughts swirled through her brain as she over-calculated the rationale and implications of the action. She was obviously attracted to him and would like nothing more than to snuggle up with that big hunk of scales and muscles every night, but by all indicators which she had seen so far, he had felt the opposite. Carefully rising to her feet, she padded away as gently as possible in search of a cafeteria or some vending machines in search of sustenance.

Ten minutes later, she returned to the two chairs to find Seamus still asleep. He was snoring ever so slightly, which she found annoying and endearing all the same. Her former broodmate had snored loudly enough to crack eggs in their nest, forcing her to often sleep outside their cave simply to get a good night's rest. But Seamus' breathing was warm and inviting, the kind of sound which she could just dream of hearing as her head rested upon his chest.

She watched him sleep for a while, only looking away as he began to stir. His head tipped to the side where hers had been only a short while ago, and his arm stretched out, softly reaching for where her body would have been. He gripped at the air, pulling his empty hand back close to him. She felt a rush of warmth flow through her, imagining what it would have been like to feel his caress. To feel his head rest down upon hers. What she would give to be back in that chair and experience these moments which only the void of her absence was lucky enough to experience.

She stood watching him for a while longer, completely lost to the concept of time. After a spell, he awoke fully, looking up at her half-asleep and smiling. It only took a moment, though, for the enchanting experience to dissipate to the aether. Once he realized where he was and what him and Maggie had been there for, he was back to the usual professional and serious Seamus. He sat up straight in the chair and planted his feet firmly on the floor beneath him.

"G'morning, Maggie," he said, clearing his throat. He stretched his arms out before him, his muscles rippling as his claws shot out toward the opposite wall. Even half-asleep and disheveled, she thought that he was gorgeous. "Did you sleep well?"

She laughed, sensing the humor in his question. "As well as one can on a hard metal folding chair in the hallway of a hospital. But the company was nice, at least."

Maggie couldn't believe that she had just said that. Looking down at her coffee cup in one hand, she decided that her brain obviously needed to wake up a little more before it tried to make words again. Taking a sip, she awkwardly thrust the other cup out to Seamus. Still staring up at her unsure of what to say, he cautiously reached up and took it from her.

They both drank their coffee for a few minutes without speaking. While a little embarrassed, she hadn't said anything untrue. She'd let him try to deny it, but for as long as it held their mutual attentions, the silence lingered.

Thankfully, a nurse materialized through Noah's door a little while later to change the subject for them. "Are you Wilhelm's next of kin?"

"No, but we're friends," Seamus said, speaking for both of them. "Wilhelm didn't have anyone else. The job was his life and the crew his family."

The nurse nodded to them both and stepped to the side, motioning for them to enter. "He's finally awake and able to speak again. He asked for Scorcher. Is that you?"

Seamus smirked and looked down to his feet. It brought Maggie joy to see some level of mirth creep back into the sweet man's face. He had been so happy that morning back on the docks but had been anything but since Wilhelm's arrival.

"Yes, that's me," Seamus admitted. "I don't really use that name anymore. It's kind of silly."

The nurse looked him up and down. "I kind of like it."

Maggie shot the female dragon a look which silently screamed that she was one more flirt away from lighting the woman up in a stream of jealousy-fueled molten death. The nurse looked back at her and shirked away.

The three of them quietly entered the room with Maggie and Seamus sitting on opposite sides of Wilhelm's gurney. The nurse closed the privacy curtain around the bed to give the three of them some time to themselves and quietly left the room. Seamus looked down at the dragon and winced.

"Don't BS me, Scorcher," Wilhelm said, his voice dry and raspy. It was clear that the dragon hadn't had any fresh water in a while and was suffering from dehydration, among other maladies. "How do I look?"

"You look like you fought Tiamat herself," Seamus finally said, after a moment of contemplation.

"Ha!" Wilhelm croaked. "That good, huh?"

The three dragons laughed. One to mask his pain; two to mask their sorrow. Wilhelm let his head drop back to the pillow and stared up at the ceiling while Maggie and Seamus looked to each other. They all knew where the conversation was going next but didn't know where, or how, to even begin.

Maggie, looking longingly at the male she loved, realized that her presence alone may hinder this moment. In order for him to fully open to the other male and talk about his wife, she couldn't be there to interfere. Standing from her chair, she looked down at Wilhelm.

"Why don't I give you two gents a moment to catch up, yeah?" she said. "Can I get either of you something to drink? A snack, maybe?"

Seamus shook his head and looked off into the far corner of the tiny room. Wilhelm looked over at his bedside table where a collection of pill bottles, water cups, and various fruits awaited him.

"Would you mind," he rasped slowly. "Would you mind grabbing some ginger ale? Human kind, if they have it. I haven't tasted that in years."

Maggie's face brightened and she grinned enthusiastically. She finally had her chance to escape while possibly helping the hurt dragon in the process. She looked to Seamus, allowing her gaze to linger. He looked back but averted his eyes just as quickly.

Maggie rose and slid her chair off to the side. Carefully

swinging her tail and wings around so as to not hit the male in the bed, she exited the room and looked around the halls for some soda.

Seamus and Wilhelm sat together quietly for a few minutes, both dragons awkwardly staring elsewhere to avoid talking. Both were glad to see one another, but neither ready to speak.

But Seamus needed to know.

Working up the courage, Seamus finally broke the silence. He cleared his throat and straightened up in the chair before beginning. His mouthed opened and then closed. He licked his lips, adjusted his wings, and did just about everything that he could imagine to delay this moment just a little further.

Summoning the last vestige of emotional strength left in his heart, Seamus finally looked back to Wilhelm in the bed and spoke.

"So, how did it happen?"

There, he said it. Seamus was ashamed of himself for jumping to conclusions and assuming the worst, but he knew that Wilhelm would have mentioned something about Matilda by now if she were still alive somewhere. Besides, the look on the other dragon's face was all the confirmation that he needed.

"I'm so sorry, Seamus," Wilhelm croaked after a moment.

"I know," he said, looking the other male in the eyes. "I know."

After another long bout of silence, one in which Wilhelm was visibly battling his inner demons, he began the tale which he had dreaded telling for years. Despite the countless nights alone in his makeshift shelter rehearsing this moment to the shadows dancing across the rough-hewn thatched walls, he still found it difficult to even open his mouth to utter the first word.

"The morning that we left port," he began, finally, "the last morning that you saw… well, you know."

Seamus looked down to the floor, unable to keep his eyes on the other dragon. He didn't blame Wilhelm for anything which transpired, but it was hard to not hate the male in this moment for the pain which he was about to cause him.

"We headed southeast out of port, looking to follow a large school of tuna which was rumored to be positioned just off the coast of Yarmouth over in Nova Scotia," he began. "Ma… Matilda was acting captain that morning, having been recently promoted for her great work the previous season. She had a knack for finding schools of fish prized by the humans and could sniff them out from miles away."

Seamus listened on, saddened by the inrush of memories stemming from the dragon's tale. His heart did warm at the thought of her skill and promotion prior to her disappearance. She loved being out at sea and hunting the elusive water creatures. Local restaurants knew that when she was out on the water that they'd be serving the best and freshest food that evening to their guests, both human and dragon alike.

"I was working the lines along with Gunnar, Einar, and Ólafur. I'm not sure if you remember them, but they were the biggest and strongest dragons in the fleet and could rig a ship with their eyes closed and one claw. It was amazing to watch them work."

Seamus shot him a look that screamed get on with it

but lacked the words to follow. He knew the dragon hadn't spoken with another of his kind in more years than he wished to remember and needed this as much as the other. He wouldn't admit it, but Seamus, while anxious to find out what had transpired, tolerated the tangential details as they allowed a moment of procrastination before the delivery of the gut-wrenching news. Sensing the other dragon's displeasure, Wilhelm refocused and continued.

"Matilda sent out our two fastest fliers, Helga and Margrét, to scout the waters ahead of us. They were nimble and strong, able to fly circles around the bulkier males and soar higher and faster than the most agile birds of prey. Helga shot straight up to look far and wide for any signs of bad weather while Margrét soared out toward the southern tip of Nova Scotia to look for any signs of the school beneath the ocean's surface."

Seamus leaned back in his chair, diving deeper into the words of Wilhelm's story as the dragon progressed. It felt good to listen to the old sailing life of his beloved. The names of her crew flooded into his mind, pushing aside years of sorrow and anguish as he was thrust backwards in years to a simpler time.

"We kept the boat on course, seeking out the hot spot that Matilda could sense just a few nautical miles away from our position. The boys kept the ship running like a top while your lass worked hand signals back and forth with Margrét as the latter swooped around the boat. She kept flying up and out, dive-bombing good-looking locations to get a sense of what was lurking just below the dark blue of the Atlantic. We ultimately made our way northeast from that position, heading north through the Gulf of Maine toward the Bay of Fundy. The course was true, and

Matilda's excitement was palpable across the deck. Everything seemed to be going great until…"

"…until what?" Seamus asked when Wilhelm simply trailed off without finishing. The dragon simply laid there in the hospital bed, staring at the wall just over Seamus' shoulder. He gulped, mustering his body to resume his courage and finish the story.

"Everything seemed to be going great until Helga came screaming down from the sky, shooting toward the rear of the ship like a meteor burning through the atmosphere. She flexed her wings on approach in a vain effort to stop, ultimately swooping around the hull. She dragged her feet across the crests of the passing waves, dropping her speed as she shot around the vessel with one more pass. Coming around, she puffed out her wings, jumped into the air a few feet, and dropped down to the deck."

"Was she alright?" Seamus asked. "Sounds like she came in way too fast."

"Yes, and yes," Wilhelm replied. "She came down so hard on the deck that she cracked the fiberglass. Matilda was pissed, and rightfully so, but the offense was quickly forgotten as Helga relayed her news."

"What did she see?"

"She had been circling high above and had been in periodic contact just to keep us apprised of the incoming weather. While we had checked the morning's weather report and saw that there would be a small storm to the east of Nova Scotia, we had left prior to seeing updates saying that strong winds from the ocean had pushed the storm west toward us. As we approached the southern tip of the peninsula, we ran smack into the front of the storm system."

Seamus grimaced and looked away. He knew the waters which Wilhelm described and could imagine having to brave strong winds and cresting waves in that region. His mind raced as he tried to picture the exact position of the boat and what he would have done in that same situation.

"We never stood a chance," Wilhelm admitted, after a moment's reflection. It was clear that he was recalling the moment in exacting details parallel to Seamus' mental conjuring. "Matilda tried her best, Seamus. You know that. But the waves were too big for our boat and the wind just never relented."

Seamus looked away, staring at nothing outside the window. He needed to hear the rest of the story but couldn't bear to do so. Wilhelm paused, giving Seamus the chance to ask him to stop. When the request failed to come, he pushed onward.

"Matilda tried cutting to the north to bring us into one of the hundreds of little natural harbors sheltered by the innumerous island hills. We had Cape Sable in sight and thought that we could have made it when a giant slammed into the side of us. I couldn't see where the hell it had come from, but it was easily twice the height of our main mast.

"Gunnar was the first to go, technically. A wave slammed into him and tossed his body from the deck. We never saw him again. I hope that the force of the wave killed him on impact because I can't imagine the alternative. And I say that he was the first technically because we never saw Margrét return from her scouting mission. I imagine that she got caught up in the wind or waves and hadn't had the time to double back before succumbing to either."

Seamus watched as several tears fell from Wilhelm's eyes. It was very rare for dragons to cry due to the hardened seals around their eyes to help protect them from their own fire breath. But it was even more rare for a male dragon to cry. Thousands of generations of masculine breeding had beaten that ability out of their sons. Not to mention that the dragon was still suffering from severe dehydration, so Seamus could hardly believe that his body would give up that much needed water.

He wanted to cry. He wanted to share in with the male's sorrow. But this was his moment to open up and experience grief with another member of his species. He had spent so long without any dragon to talk to. Anyone to console in. Besides, Seamus had cried a lifetime's worth of tears years ago.

"Over the next hour," the dragon finally continued after composing himself, "We lost almost everyone else."

The tears still trickled down through the cracks in his scales, only more slowly now. The parched keratin wicked the moisture from view, absorbing the water faster than gravity could lay claim to the falling droplets.

"Helga, having exhausted her strength flying high above the clouds for us, could barely hold on to the rigging to keep herself stable. She was flung overboard as a wave nearly toppled the ship. I swear I saw the keel breach the water's surface at one point, we were hit so hard. Her body slammed into the decking as the boat lurched and a wave took care of the rest.

"With the islands in sight, we thought that we might have finally made it. That is, until the ship crashed into the rocks. We never saw them coming, but they split the hull in twain and threw us all this way and that. It was during this moment where everything went to shit.

"Matilda was thrown into a hole in the deck and bashed against splintered fiberglass and decking. She suffered multiple broken bones and both of her wings were severed completely. Einar suffered similarly, and Ólafur was pulled under the water and out of sight. We never saw him after that and assumed that he was pulled down with the wreckage. It was only through the combined efforts of our swimming that we managed to regroup and escaped the sinking wreckage. As the remains of our floating home disappeared into the murky darkness below, we swam for our lives toward the closest piece of land that we could see.

"I don't know for sure, but it felt like we had swum for hours. It could have been five minutes, for all I know. I was pretty banged up through all of that and given that we couldn't see much beyond a wingspan away, we were happy just to finally feel hard earth under our claws again."

Seamus reached out and gripped the male's bony, frail hand. The palm was covered in raw callouses, the clawed fingers stronger than one could believe. It was evident that Wilhelm had spent his years working nonstop with little nutrition to replace his spent calories. Wilhelm squeezed, looking back to him.

"So, how did you survive?

"By the grace of Tiamat and the determination of your wife," Wilhelm answered, straightening up in the bed. "We were all ready to give up, but she wouldn't let us. The three of us were battered and broken with little to show for it, but we had our spirits and most of our functional limbs to fight and survive.

"We all had lost or damaged our wings in the process, so none of us could fly. The nearest island was barely in sight, and we could hardly swim to shore, let alone brave the waters once more to get to another island which may or may not have some dragon on it to save us. So, we stayed on that first island."

Seamus looked down, resting the tip of his snout upon his chest. He was mentally calculating the remaining dragons, their physical ailments, and the available resources. The grim reality of what they had faced was apparent and quickly dashed any hopes which he may have had of her surviving for very long.

"As you can imagine, my friend, things were pretty bleak. We tried making some signal fires, but there wasn't much dry material to burn and there was very little food. Working together, we were able to set up some rain catches to get fresh water and hunted what little we could find around the island in the shallows.

"Given his injuries, Einar didn't last long. He passed a few days later and we buried him under a pile of stones on the west side of the island, away from the wind. It was the nicest place on the land, as it was comforting to sit and stare off into the distance, imagining that we could see our homes and loved ones back here in Maine. I sat there for countless hours just staring and hoping that maybe, just maybe, they were looking back at us."

A tear crept out from the edge of Seamus' left eye but was quickly wiped away. He knew where this was going next and couldn't bear to hear the words.

"She talked about you," Wilhelm said, breaking Seamus from his reverie. "Nonstop. She made plans of how to get back, how to return us to the mainland to see you again. Tiamat, it was almost annoying at times how much she loved you. She'd wouldn't shut up."

Both dragons chuckled at that, a welcome break from the despondency which had enveloped their reunion thus far.

"Her love for you is what kept her going for as long as she did, and her determination to get back to you is what kept me motivated to live. But it wasn't enough. We both sat there, unable to fly, too hurt to swim, and seemingly too far away from all of civilization, even though we knew it was just over the horizon.

"I would like to give you more details, but much of that time began to blur. I couldn't begin to tell you what date she had passed on as we'd stopped recording days by that point. But it was a beautiful day. Sunny, only a little rain, and a gentle crashing of waves on the oceanside of the island."

Wilhelm laughed to himself, receiving a confused look from Seamus who was deep in thought.

"I'm sorry," he croaked, taking a sip of water. "I'm not laughing at her dying; I'm laughing at my perception of nice weather. Days without rain meant that we had nothing to drink. Our ideal weather on the island was a gentle enough rainstorm to fill our bellies and water tanks without being miserable."

Seamus nodded in understanding. He had never been in that situation before but could easily comprehend the dragon's notion. It was strange how your environment and situation could change you.

"So, I buried her on the beach alongside Einar. I can take you there sometime if you like. After she passed... I didn't know what to do with myself. I eventually dug a third grave, right up against hers so that we could be touching, just in case."

Wilhelm suddenly stopped and looked away from Seamus. It had been comforting to finally talk to another dragon after all that time. It had been nice to open up to the other dragon with tears in his eyes, knowing how much of an impact he was having on someone's life after all these years.

But he couldn't look at Seamus anymore. The tears in the other dragon's eyes had all but dried up, baked away by the fire burning within. The eyes, smoldering with anger and hatred, staring down at the dragon in the hospital bed.

"What did you say?" Seamus finally uttered after an uncomfortably long silence.

"Uh—nothing, I was rambling. I don't know, it's been years since I've spoken to another sapient creature, Seamus. I'm dehydrated and delirious."

Seamus cleared his throat and stood up from the chair. He towered over Wilhelm in the small bed and stared down at his withered form.

"You wanted to… touch her… in death."

"I'm sorry!" Wilhelm screamed. The voice ruptured from his cracked throat, painfully tearing itself from the bowels of the emaciated dragon. "I… I… I loved her, Seamus."

Silence.

"I loved her," he muttered, looking into the dragon's eyes, pleading with him to understand. "You don't know what it was like! You don't know what it was like to be alone on that island with no contact with the outside world. All that I had was her! For all we knew, we would never see another soul again. And even when I finally told her how I felt, she kept going on and on about how much she loved you and that you'd be reunited someday. Agh! Tiamat, she could be so infuriating at times."

What had started as a small trickle of tears leading to a slow simmer of anger, had finally boiled over. All the anger, hatred, sorrow, misery, and ten-thousand other blurry emotions overlapping like some pit of vipers melding into each other as they wriggled and swirled through Seamus' brain burst forth like pent up magma pressurized beneath the Earth's crust.

The quiet, typically reserved dragon turned toward the window, whipping his tail around with him. The chair, taking the full force of his strong, meaty appendage flew across the room, shattering to splinters against the far wall. His chest heaved as his breathing intensified. Smoke swirled from his nostrils, billowing clouds of acrid haze up toward the ceiling.

Seamus turned back toward the bed and glared at Wilhelm. His eyes glowed brightly as raging blood rushed through his veins, filling his orbs with hatred and malice. Arms at his sides, he flicked them sharply, extended the knife-like claws from each hand, poised to slash and rake the other dragon's body to shreds.

Wilhelm stared up in horror at Seamus looming over him. Even if he had wanted to flee, he was in too weakened of a state to move quickly enough to evade the predator. His life hung in the balance, to be decided by the wronged husband of his long-lost love. Wilhelm closed his eyes, leaned his head back, and exposed his neck to the other. He would accept whatever fate Seamus decided for him.

The thin tendrils of smoke, now a steady stream of dark grey puffs rushing toward the top of the bed chamber, finally built enough strength and found their way to the smoke detector. The device, sensing the acrid smoke roiling upward from Seamus' throat, fired a signal off to the fire alarm controls in the main computer room of the hospital. Red lights strobed as a piercing wail filled the dead air of the otherwise quiet hospital wing.

Gripping his skull, the shrill sounds of the alarm burrowed their way into Seamus' ears and assaulted his brain with pulsating agony. He had never been one for loud noises and preferred the quiet solitude of life on his isolated lighthouse in the sea. Caught between the feeling of his head exploding, his blinding hatred of the man before him, and the raging sorrow for his wife, something snapped deep within Seamus.

Looking down at Wilhelm, he bared his teeth and let loose a blood curdling roar. The man's sheets, the morning's newspaper, and various medical devices around the bed, flew back and slammed into the chamber's wall with the fury of the roar. Seamus spun around toward the window and let loose the fiery salvo which had been building within him for the injured dragon at his side.

Lighting his promethium glands, Seamus breathed a roaring plume of burning hatred toward the glass and wood portal in front of him, blasting millions of razor-thin shards of burning debris outward and to the ground below. Pushing off with his feet, he flung himself through the window, smashing what had remained from his onslaught. Dragon, window, and bits of trim flew out into the cool morning air and faded into the fog-covered forest floor below.

CHAPTER XVI

"So, have you talked to Seamus lately?" the dragon asked Maggie, tossing her a line.

She deftly caught the coil with one hand, gripped an end, and heaved it up and over the mast. Maggie had done this countless times now and could do it with her eyes closed. In fact, she knew pretty much every inch of this ship by now and could sail circles around most of the other novices in Bar Harbor.

After sailing for most of the Fall with the man and helping him repair a few of the boats in his fleet over the cold winter months, Captain Rex enthusiastically offered her a spot on his crew. Granted, he made her take his grueling two-week training course as soon as the waters warmed up, but she didn't mind. She got to sail in his Trapper 501 and loved every minute of it. Maggie had been hesitant to head out on the water so often given her job with Sparu, but she had negotiated the hours with both of her bosses and sorted things out. Working mostly on the weekdays for Rexforth and Sparu on the weekends when tourists were staying in the campground, she had quickly settled into a comfortable routine to balance out the hours.

Turning back to face the other dragon after catching the coil of rope falling down the other side, she looked up at him as she knotted the line to a deck cleat. "No, not lately. Why, you haven't? I thought that you two were friends?"

"And I thought that you two were friends," he countered.

"Well, he's been kind of weird lately and I've been super busy with work. Between me never being around and him being aloof, and downright angry looking at times, we just haven't really been talking."

"What do you mean, lately?" he asked, eying her from across the deck. "Did, uh, something happen?"

"I don't know," she replied, looking back at him, now just a little suspicious. "I guess if I had to pick a day, I'd say it was around when you showed up."

Wilhelm glared at her without responding. They spent the rest of the morning working silently, keep the ship sailing smoothly under the careful watch of their captain. If the man noticed that something was amiss, he either didn't understand or understood all too well to say anything about it. Maggie assumed the latter.

Maggie, walking across the deck, crouched down next to the wheel. Closing her eyes, she basked in the warm sun caressing the scales of her face, loving the springtime mix of temperatures flitting across her body as the cool ocean breeze gusted into them. Looking down to her side, she smiled at the man steering the ship.

"You look happy, lass," Captain Rex said. "What are you up to?"

Grinning sheepishly, she pointed out toward the Narrows ahead of them. "I see that we're bearing north instead of tacking over to the east to head back to port," she said, her smile broadening. "Are we going anywhere in particular?"

The captain smiled with her now, happy to see her so

full of joy. He had high hopes for the two dragons and had been dismayed when rumors floated around about the incident back at the hospital. Seamus had rarely been seen since the Fall after smashing a hole through the side of the hospital. Few dragons or humans claimed to have seen him about town, and even then, it was usually just to pick up supplies before heading back to the lighthouse.

"You might say that," he replied, winking.

Maggie, full of a renewed pep despite the long day on the cold water, ran from this and that on the deck, securing lines and preparing the ship for the next leg of the journey. She had taken on her new responsibilities with great vigor and had come to learn every nook and cranny on the ship. Captain Rex would often be about to yell out a command to her, only to find Maggie already on top of the task and staying one step ahead of his orders. She had turned into a fine executive officer aboard his ships, and he was lucky to have her.

"What are you so happy about?" Wilhelm asked Maggie as she flitted from place to place.

"Oh, nothing," she said, blushing. "Just enjoying our voyage and looking forward to having my feet back on solid ground."

The other dragon watched her suspiciously, clearly not buying it. He strolled down the deck to the wheel and stood adjacent to the captain. Wilhelm waited until he was sure that Maggie might not be listening and leaned in closer to the captain.

"So, what's up with her?"

Captain Rex eyed him curiously. "Maggie? Oh, she just enjoys sailing on these beautiful waters in the great state of Maine, that's all. And she really likes big, erect phallic structures protruding from the water."

Wilhelm rolled his eyes and walked away. The captain laughed into the wind knowing that he was getting under the new recruit's skin. He wasn't one hundred percent sure just what had happened back there in the hotel room where Wilhelm was recuperating after his return, but he knew that something had gone down between the two males. And after all of his years of friendship with the lighthouse keeper, he knew which side of the argument he'd be on once the truth emerged. But, he had needed help with some upcoming runs and decided to give the dragon a chance.

Calling out to his two deck hands to drop the sails, he brought the ship around to the leeward side of the rocky outcropping forming the foundation for the lighthouse. Wilhelm dropped the anchor from its perch and watched the heavy iron object splash into the waves, disappearing down below into the dark waters of the Atlantic. He'd normally get excited about a delivery to such a historic building, but this one didn't spark joy in his life anymore.

Gripping the crate in her clawed hands, Maggie pushed off from the deck and beat her wings against the southernly wind. Pumping furiously to gain altitude, she slowly brought herself up and around to the gallery's catwalk. There, at the top and waiting for her arrival, was Seamus.

"Maggie," he said, nodding curtly, with a strained smile. She wasn't sure if it was forced or just difficult for him to muster, but she was happy to see it regardless.

"Good day, Seamus," she said, returning the smile and beaming at him. "We had a good run today and Captain Rexforth said that you might be hankering some fish."

She held out the crate for him to grab, flying backward

as he accepted it to put some distance between her and the stone walls of the lighthouse. While she'd like nothing more than to have the beating wind drive her into the arms of the male, she was still keeping her distance since the event at the hospital. Seamus had never said goodbye that day, nor explained himself after the fact. All that Maggie knew was that it wasn't her fault and that she should just wait for him to come back to her when he was ready.

And ready she was. More than ready.

Giving him one last smile with that girlish, toothy grin that she developed whenever she saw him as of late, Maggie wrapped her wings around herself and plummeted down to the water. Throwing them outward a dozen feet above the water's surface, she billowed her wings out and above her body, catching the air and slowing her drop to the deck of the boat. Dropping to the fiberglass and wood below, she plunged the bow of the ship down into the drink as the vessel compensated for her rapidly added mass.

Wilhelm shot her a dirty look, both for her fondness around Seamus and nearly tossing him from the deck with her acrobatic display. Rex merely gave her a wink and laughed again, his raucous voice disappearing with the torrent of air whipping across the surface of the ship.

Looking up to the male above, Captain Rex gave the lighthouse keeper a crisp salute. With his returned nod from above, Rexforth motioned to Wilhelm to retrieve the anchor and prepared his vessel for departure. Calling to Maggie to stop staring at the lighthouse keeper and to get back to work, he could see Wilhelm struggling with the anchor down the far end.

"Wilhelm, me boy, what's wrong?"

"I don't know, sir" the dragon replied. "The chain is

stuck. It won't budge!"

The captain locked the wheel in place and shuffled down the deck, muttering something about rusty chains and out of shape deckhands. He watched the dragon pull on the chain for a moment, perplexed as to why it would seem to give a little, then drop down another five feet or so. This kept happening for several moments before a thought crossed the captain's smaller, human mind.

The chain looks like a fishing line with an awfully big fish toying with it.

"Maggie!" Captain Rex hollered. "Disconnect the windlass. Drop that chain now!"

"Drop the chain into the ocean? Isn't that bad for the environment?" she asked, legitimately concerned. "What's wrong over there?"

"Please, lass, just do it. I'll explain later!"

Seeing Maggie shrug her shoulders in concession, the captain turned back to the chain disappearing into the water below. He looked to the dragon deckhand and was about to speak when he felt something pulling on his prosthetic leg. The ship lurched downward, and he would have fallen in had Wilhelm not reached out and grabbed him by an arm.

Looking down at his immobilized leg, he found that his suspicions were correct and that his horror had come true. Biting down on the side of his boat, with his leg included, was the biggest hydrolisk he had ever seen. The thing released and bit again, this time digging into the flesh of the captain's remaining leg. The man howled in pain as the creature's teeth sank deeper.

Descended from dragons who had taken to the sea many generations before, hydrolisks appeared similar to classical dragons in that they had four limbs, a head, tail, and two wings. Where they differed, however, was that webbing had developed between their claws over time and that their wings had shrunk and tapered back toward their tails. The wings functioned more as control rudders to aid in maneuvering under water, and some human biologists believed they could no longer fly on them if they had tried.

Their scales, while analogous to those of Wilhelm, Maggie, and their ilk, evolved to secrete a mucous-like substance which helped them to move more smoothly through the open ocean. Additionally, a small section of their necks had developed gills to allow the dragons to breathe underwater, while still breathing in air through their mouths on land. The combination of their traditional body features and the newly acquired characteristics made hydrolisks truly terrifying creatures.

"Chain release in three, two, one," Maggie counted down to warn the others. "Chain is free!"

The beginning of the chain shot free from the windlass, whipping down the channel and out the side of the hull. It was then that she finally looked up and saw the top of the dragon's snout protruding from the edge of the deck. The captain's face, a mixture of pain, surprise, and sheer horror, was burned into her eyes more deeply than even the hottest dragonbreath could hope for. Turning to her left, she looked back to the lighthouse, hoping to Tiamat that he was still there.

"SEAMUS!"

Not waiting for a reply, she bolted to the stern, leaping over various pieces of rigging and decking which stood in her way. Racing to the edge of the vessel, she leapt over the side, aiming squarely for the face of the hydrolisk.

Splashing into the frothy waves below, she grappled with the larger dragon's head, gripping its upper jaw with her hands and pushing downward with her legs on the lower.

She struggled against the vise-like jaws of the aquatic hunter, hoping against all hope that she could wrench the creature's jaws free long enough for Captain Rex to free his leg from its grasp. Feeling her claws dig into the gums of the creature, she channeled all her strength and raw power into her muscles, pushing the hydrolisk's jaws apart.

"Wilhelm!" she grunted between her clenched teeth. "Pull the captain free and get him out of here!"

After hearing no reply and still seeing Rexforth's bleeding leg in front of her, she looked up to see the other dragon clambering clear of the hydrolisk and further up the deck. Straining against the might of the bigger dragon, she heaved again, pushing its jaw up and over the decking of the ship.

"Rex! Can you hear me!?" she screamed.

He didn't answer. She wasn't even sure if he was still moving or not. Freeing one hand, she pulled down on the human's leg, ripping it free of the hydrolisk's tooth. A sickly sucking sound popped into her ears as the muscle and flesh of the tiny human's body slide from the pearly white tooth, his body falling to the deck. Reaching over, she grabbed the captain about his middle and threw his body higher onto the tilting deck of the boat.

Looking back to the hydrolisk, she stared down into the maw of the beast. Its tongue swished from side to side, slapping against her leg as it tried to find whatever it was that was holding its jaws apart. Seeing her only chance to buy them some time, she sucked in a deep breath, primed her promethium glands, and unleashed hell into the mouth of the dragon. Not waiting for its response, she pushed off from its lower jaw and leapt back onto the deck.

As her feet connected, the boat tilted further as the hydrolisk recovered from her assault and was once again chomping down onto the fiberglass shell. The body of the captain, who she couldn't tell was alive or dead at this point, slid toward her. Holding onto one of the deck cleats, she reached out and grabbed him up with her free hand, saving him from the awaiting jaws of the hungry water dragon.

Looking around, she tried to calculate her odds of survival. Her body ached from the attack on the hydrolisk, the captain was unconscious at best, and Wilhelm, well, he was nowhere to be seen. Putting all of her known variables together, she realized that trying to fly away was her only option at this point.

Pumping with all her remaining might, she was about to take flight when she felt the teeth crunch through the membranes of one of her wings She screamed in pain, struggling to maintain her grip on the deck cleat and the captain's body. Unsure of what to do next, she looked to the sky in hopes of an answer.

It wasn't Tiamat who answered her, though. It was a mere mortal who had eyes only for her.

"Give me your hand!" Seamus bellowed as he crashed to the angled deck. His claws dug into the fiberglass hull, holding him steady as he swung his arms down to the female. His wings were kept deployed, balancing his body and preparing for the extra load he was about to carry.

"I'm fine!" she lied, as the hydrolisk repositioned its jaws, opening and quickly closing back down into the side of the fishing vessel. "Take him!"

She heaved the captain's lifeless form toward Seamus,

trusting blindly in his ability to catch the human in time. He reached out, grabbing at the captain with one hand while holding onto the mast with the other.

"Go!" she called. "I'll be fine. Get him to safety and come back for us after."

With a solemn nod, Seamus relented. He pushed off from the deck and beat his wings against the cool ocean air, rising into the sky toward the lighthouse.

"Are you crazy!" Wilhelm screamed at Maggie. He had spent the past few moments clambering higher up the mast away from the creature below. "Why did you let him leave us? We're going to get eaten. We're going to die because of you!"

The hydrolisk bit into the side of the ship again, taking a chunk of fiberglass with it. Finally given the chance, the Atlantic poured through the hole, filling the inside of the vessel with cold sea water. The ship began to list as the bow fell deeper into the water. The stern rose into the air and Wilhelm began to slip down the wet surface of the tilting mast and onto the deck.

"You bitch! You know that I can't fly. Where is that jerk when you need him." Wilhelm struggled to climb the surface of the ship. The stern continued to rise up further above the ocean's surface, nearing forty-five degrees into the air. "He never deserved Matilda, and he certainly doesn't deserve you. I'll see to that."

Looking down at Maggie struggling to free herself from the wreckage of the ship as she tried to wrench herself free from the jaws of the hydrolisk, Wilhelm dug his claws into the deck and slid down, landing squarely on Maggie's head and neck. He kicked at her face, desperately trying to free her from the side of the ship and send her into the maw of their attacker. If he could just give the dragon what it wanted, perhaps it would leave him alone…

It was then that the foot connected with his face. Reeling back from the kick, he looked through blurry eyes to see Seamus a wingspan away and holding onto the sideways mast.

"Leave her alone!" Seamus bellowed, having seen the other dragon's actions as he flew back from the lighthouse. "You took one female away from me. You won't take another."

Launching himself forward, he plowed into Wilhelm's chest, raking his scales with claws and teeth. Seamus, a normally calm and reserved creature of service to his fellow dragon and humankind, reverted to his primal instincts and unleashed his pent-up rage against the other. He hacked and slashed, blocking each and every attempt from Wilhelm to fight back and protect himself. Seamus attacked with blind rage, clawing at vulnerable areas as they presented themselves.

Wilhelm, bleeding from a dozen wounds, let go of his hold on the deck and slid down to attack Maggie once again. He knew that he couldn't take Seamus on in a fair fight but calculated that he could get into the other's head by going after Maggie. Love makes dragons do strange things, and it might just be the distraction that he needed. Pulling back a foot to kick her once more, he looked up to watch for Seamus' obvious attack.

But he was looking in the wrong direction. The attack came from below.

Not needing a male to rescue her, Maggie, still holding back the hydrolisk from attacking them or the boat, jumped upward and clawed at Wilhelm's abdomen. Racking his scales, she drove her claws from his navel down to his right thigh. Relishing in the screeching wail of pain escaping Wilhelm's mouth, she cocked her head back, warmed her promethium glands, and set the dragon on fire.

Timing her actions, she let go of the Hydrolisk's head and launched herself up and past Wilhelm's writhing body. She pushed off his shoulders, driving him downward as she raced up and grabbed on to the mast next to Seamus. The look of surprise on his face spoke volumes, and she almost felt bad about ruining his chivalrous plans for coming to her rescue.

"What's the matter? Did you think that I needed you to rescue me like some damsel in distress?"

"Well, I, uh—" he stammered.

She leaned forward and kissed him on the cheek. Smiling, she let go of the mast, stretching her wings as she soared over the hydrolisk and out and around the sinking wreckage of the captain's fishing vessel. Seamus' eyed her departure, grinning as he watched her lithe yet strong body fly over the crashing waves. He looked down once more to watch the tip of a tail disappear into the maw of the sea dragon below. The creature, obviously having its fill of meat for one sitting and realizing that the additional effort of catching the other two dragons wasn't worth it, eyed Seamus above before dropping back into the water, never to be seen again.

Seamus dropped from the horizontal mast and swooped through the air. Beating his wings, he rode the strong currents racing across the surface of the water and struggled to catch up with Maggie. He looked over his shoulder one last time on his way back to the lighthouse, mourning the loss of the ship.

"How is he?" Seamus asked, looking up from his book.

It had been a long night. The captain, while overall in fairly good shape, had lost a lot of blood from the dragon's tooth to his leg. The end of his already amputated leg had been mangled by the hungry hydrolisk and was barely recognizable by the time both Maggie and Seamus had returned to the lighthouse. Sensing that he needed a human-run hospital to treat his wounds, Maggie had flown him to the closest one on the mainland while Seamus remained behind to run the lighthouse... and watch the waters for the returning creature.

Maggie had stayed with him, hovering outside his open window as she couldn't fit inside the building designed for only humans, until the doctors were able to return him to a stable condition. It was just past midnight when she returned, happy to find Seamus still up and waiting for her.

"He'll be okay," she said, shaking her wings and tail on the catwalk surrounding the gallery. Seamus rose to meet her. "But the doctors think that he'll lose a little more of the leg. That hydrolisk really did a number on him."

Seamus grimaced, but then smiled. "Well, knowing Rexforth, he'll probably find the positive in the situation and be happy that he can finally buy a new leg for the occasion. Maybe he'll even get a real peg leg like a sea captain of olde."

Maggie snorted, trying in vain to hold back her

laughter. It was kind of mean to speak in jest about their dear friend so soon after his accident, but she had to admit that it was probably true.

"Are you hungry?" Seamus asked, motioning toward the hatch leading down to his living quarters. "I have some tea on the stove and could make up some sandwiches or something else if you like."

Maggie grinned slyly, thinking beyond the words which were spoken. He had just invited her downstairs to his home. It was well past midnight, and he was offering her a stimulating drink. Granted, her blood was still pumping furiously from the attack on the ship and the fight with Wilhelm, so she probably wouldn't fall asleep any time soon, but she would love to lay down in bed and relax for a change. Maybe that's what he had in mind, too.

"I'd like that."

An hour later, the two dragons sat on a modest couch in Seamus' living quarters. Given the nature of lighthouse design, all of the rooms were round or shared curved walls with other rooms, lacked a ton of spacious room to really move around, and limited the creativity of decoration. Looking around the room, Maggie could tell that Seamus had lived alone for quite some time and the lighthouse's décor could benefit from a woman's touch.

Pushing her plate forward on the coffee table, Maggie leaned back into the plush cushions and rested her head. Staring up at the ceiling, she contemplated her future and how this view of the lighthouse might play a part. Would she never see this room again, or might she find herself in a position to return here often, resting on this very couch in more intimate scenarios?

Turning to her left, she looked longingly at the male

next to her. They weren't quite touching but were only separated by a few inches on the adjacent cushions. She cared about him, and he about her, that was obvious, but where would this relationship go? Would they continue to flit around each other like butterflies on a breezy day, constantly near one another but never getting close enough for something deeper and more meaningful to transpire?

Gazing into his eyes, she half expected him to be falling asleep and drifting off after such a long and eventful day. But between the tea and his lifelong habits of manning the lighthouse throughout the dangerous dark nights of coastal Maine, his eyes shone bright and vibrant against the faint glow of the nearby candles.

"Maggie—"

"Yes, Seamus?" she responded, cutting him off. She was so excited to hear him speak after such a long period of silence that she couldn't help herself. She would listen to him read his grocery list at this point if only to hear his words flow melodically into her ears.

"I, um, need to explain some things," he began. "For starters, I'm sorry about what happened back at the hospital. I should have never left like a I did, especially by not saying goodbye to you first."

"I think the hospital would agree," Maggie said, with a wink.

"Yes, I know," he replied, sighing. "I've been helping their contractor with the work and still have a bill to pay before the end of the month. But back to the point. I'm not sure what you heard about our conversation, but Wilhelm revealed many things about my wife, his apparent infatuation with her, and how she died. While I was expecting half of that information, his love for her drove me mad and I couldn't control myself."

"Nobody's judging you, Seamus," she replied, reaching over and grabbing his hand. She gave it a firm, but gentle squeeze. He returned in kind. Neither let go. "And you don't owe me an explanation for anything."

"I do, though," he said, staring into her eyes. She could sit here all night just looking deeply into those pools of stars, as long as they kept looking back into hers. "I've spent years now waiting for my wife to return, knowing full well that I would never see her again. I just felt that if I didn't continue my vigil, that if I didn't continue holding on to hope for her imminent return, that I was killing her myself. I felt that if I kept watch on the sea, that if I never stopped loving her, she would stand a chance and return to me after all this time."

"Oh, Seamus, you don't have to—"

"Please, let me finish," he said, cutting her off. "It's not fair to you and it's not fair to me. You've been nothing but kind to me and I've pushed you away at every chance. The fact that you've stuck with me this long says that you're either crazy or crazy for me. I hope for the latter as it's how I feel, but until now, I haven't had the guts to admit to you, let alone myself.

"I don't know if Captain Rex ever told you, but we went out on countless exploratory missions. We searched every island, every cove, and anywhere in between where we thought that we might find some trace of her. After years of searching with nothing to show for it, I eventually cut off all ties with everyone I ever knew and retreated to my watery stronghold here out in the middle of the Narrows.

"I am not going to lie; I will never stop loving Matilda.

I loved her for more years than I can count, and she's burned into the very fiber of my being. But I don't think that she'd want me to live on like this. What I'm trying to say, Maggie, is that I love her and will never forget what we had, but I'm ready to live my life again and build the future which I deserve. And, if you'd want it, I'd like you to be a part of that—"

Before he had a chance to finish, Maggie launched herself across the short gap between them and pressed her lips to his. Her arms shot forward, claws searching his body, and his searching hers. They embraced each other, giving in to their bottled-up desires which had been simmering and pressurizing for close to a year now. The two dragons threw all caution to the wind, diving into each other with no reverence for their sensuous yet deadly bodies. Claws, teeth, and even fire slashed and writhed as Maggie and Seamus gave in to their primal urges, satisfying their lust and desire for one another at long last.

EPILOGUE

Staring out at the vast waters of the Atlantic Ocean, Maggie gripped the railing on the catwalk surrounding the Crabtree Ledge Lighthouse. The sun was rising over the east, shedding its beautiful light on the vast wilderness of Maine. She had watched the sunrise countless times over the past year since her arrival, but for some reason, this one seemed different.

Feeling a burst of wind coming in from the south, she wrapped her wings around herself, hoping to stave off the bitter chill. She shivered, still feeling the cool, crisp air evade her coverage and slip underneath the membranes of her wings, threatening to sap her naked body beneath of its warmth.

That is, until she felt another set of wings moving around her. The larger set, deep red and full of life, enclosed her smaller frame and protected her from the icy winds blowing in off the cresting ocean waves. She leaned her head back, delighting in the feel of her scales pressing against his prominent pectoral muscles. Maggie cradled the back of her head between them, loving the feeling of his body so close to hers.

Turning her head, she looked up into his eyes and melted as she found him to already be looking down into hers. She gave into his embrace and allowed him to fully envelop her. Before she knew what was happening, she felt his arms scoop her smaller body up and into his. He turned back toward the gallery and headed for the stairs leading down below.

She had come up here eager to fly out to sea and hunt for some breakfast, but she hadn't counted on Seamus wanting seconds of their midnight snack. Raising her head to his, she found his kiss already waiting for her, and gave into their lust for one another.

ACKNOWLEDGEMENTS

As usual, this book would not be possible without the love and support of my wife, Kristin. Thank you for continuing to put up with my shenanigans and newly formed writing plans on a daily basis.

Thanks to Jamie Noble Frier for bringing my silly ideas to life and not laughing in my face when I pitch my own hand-drawn concept art to you.

Thanks to Ellie at Creative Digital Studios for her never-ending tips and tricks in writing and publishing, graphic design work, and for making all the puzzle pieces of this book come to life.

Thanks to Daniel Willis for making me look like I know how to spell words and use them in the proper manner.

A big thanks goes out to Cathryn Parry for her help during development and guiding me on the right path while writing my first romance / women's lit novel. And thank you to Kristin and Stephen for your help in beta reading and providing feedback.

And last but not least, thanks to YOU the reader, for supporting my writing and sticking with me over the years. Thanks!

ABOUT THE AUTHOR

Tim Baird spends his days lost in the world of medical device design and manufacturing. Volunteering with children in several youth robotics programs, he is trying his hardest to avoid growing up, one robot at a time. When he's not designing or writing, he enjoys time at home with his wife & son, watching/reading anything Star Wars related, and spending time out in the woods of New England.

CPSIA information can be obtained
at www.ICGtesting.com
Printed in the USA
BVHW081447010822
643531BV00006B/143

9 781088 038956